When Chicks Hatch

To my amazingly
cool friend, Monica
Love,
Heather Randall

When Chicks Hatch

a novel

Heather Randall

WinePressPublishing
Your Book, Defined. Since 1991.

WinePress Publishing (PO Box 428, Enumclaw, WA 98022) functions only as book publisher. As such, the ultimate design, content, editorial accuracy, and views expressed or implied in this work are those of the author.

ISBN 13: 978-1-4141-1432-3
ISBN 10: 1-4141-1432-X
Library of Congress Catalog Card Number: 2009903133

Acknowledgments

GOD PLACED A powerful story into my heart and mind. I have been blessed on this journey with many people who have loved me enough to encourage my dream.

A special thanks to…

My awesome mom: for spurring me on when I wanted to quit, and believing in the potential of this story.

Katrina and Sara: I love you both for nagging me when my procrastination set in, and inspiring me to pick up my pen again.

Erin: you're a great friend, and I appreciate that you made time in your busy life to type my manuscript.

Thanks to everyone at WinePress Publishing/Pleasant Word for their encouragement and direction.

Thanks to Chloe, Caibry, Nevie, and Sadie for letting Mommy write, and for being proud of me even when I spent all day in my pajamas.

To my husband Stan: thank you for leading me to the depth of God's grace and being patient while I learn the power of forgiveness and the richness of love. I'll drink Coke with you 'til death do us part.

Thanks to those who picked up this book, whoever you are.

This is my prayer for you:

May the love of God be your nesting place; may the light of His Word be your life source. Covered under His wings, may you grow and mature, and may His unwavering presence bring you freedom. Amen

Chapter One

THE INSTRUCTIONS WERE explicit. Term papers were to be pushed under the door of room 201 no later than 9 AM on Monday morning to receive credit. Nicky Bell smiled as she sauntered down the hall, away from room 201. She had slid her paper under the door as the clock struck ten.

Any normal student would have lost sleep—and hair—rushing down the hall, in pajamas if necessary, to get there on time. She had arrived in red Adidas joggers with snaps up the legs and a form-fitting red top. Her hair was pulled into a ponytail at the nape of her neck, one long strand of hair wrapped around the band. She was even wearing make-up.

Thick, black eyeliner clumped in her lashes, creating a dramatic contrast to her blonde hair. Her lipstick matched her shirt exactly. She enjoyed being late, enjoyed sending the message that she would not be controlled. She loved the power-rush of pushing limits. Besides, she would get an A on her paper. He had to give her one. She could afford to take her time.

Now that she thought about it, though, she did have a lot to do today. She walked past a dozen of her peers in the hall, greeting no one. She wasn't here for friendship.

She found a pop machine at the end of the hall and placed quarters through the slot and waited for something cold to drop to the bottom.

Nicky popped back the tab and took a refreshing sip as she exited the building and walked back into the fresh morning air.

She set her pop on the roof of the car as she fiddled with the key to unlock the door.

Her car door dropped a little as she opened it. That always concerned her—what if it came off in her hand one day when she opened it? What if the door suddenly wouldn't shut? She had a bungee cord under the driver's seat in case that ever happened. She didn't have the details worked out on how the bungee cord would be useful, but she felt confident something would come to her should the need arise. She was prepared for anything, and she needed no one.

Nicky reached up from her seat and removed her pop from the car roof and set it in the car's drink holder. She adjusted her radio station to a familiar tune and made her way out of the college parking lot.

Nicky turned off the radio as she pulled into her empty carport at the Walton Manor Apartments—the building marked 117A. Daryl, her neighbor across the hall, had just stomped out a cigarette, so he waited to hold the door for her.

"How 'ya doin'? Ever finish that report you were working on?"

"Just turned it in. We'll see what happens." She smiled, knowing there was no mystery about what would happen.

She unlocked her door, nodded him away, and stepped inside. The silence embraced her. It never failed. Every time she walked into her apartment she felt like spreading her arms wide and spinning in the middle of the living room. It was all hers! No cat, dog, hamster, or goldfish. She had provided this all on her own and shared credit with no one.

She hated leaving it, even if it was for only a few days. There was no one inside these walls to judge her. She could cry if she wanted to—if there was anything to cry about.

Her clothes were all laid out on the bed next to the open suitcase. *I wonder why I didn't just pack everything this morning.* She inspected each item as she placed it in the suitcase. Three basic scoop-neck shirts—one in red, one in blue, and one in purple; a gray, zip-up hoodie in case it got cold; and jeans, one black pair and one blue.

There were five pairs of white tube socks in case her feet got wet. Nothing worse than soggy socks. Aqua Net, curling iron. *I wonder if*

Jennifer will have a blow dryer? Her hair is so curly it probably has to air-dry. Better be safe and bring it.

If she could fit everything into just one bag she wouldn't have to pack a carry-on. She could use the extra time to sleep. She squeezed in her purple cosmetics bag, already packed with her toothbrush and other toiletries.

She heard the door bang in the hallway. That would be the mailman leaving the building. She darted out to her mailbox. There were three letter-sized envelopes—two were medical bills and one was an envelope addressed to Nicole Joy Bell. She hated seeing her full name spelled out like that, especially handwritten. She never used her middle name and had always preferred Nicky to Nicole. The envelope bore no return address. Who could this be from? She heard the answering machine beep as she walked back inside, and she hit the button.

"Hey, Nicky, you there? Guess not. Umm, I'm calling about the assistant mentorship with Professor Marks. I don't know why, but I just found out. Call me, okay? I'll be here till eight. Bye." The long beep followed.

"Okay, that was weird," Nicky said out loud to the phone as she dialed Becky Cunningham's office line.

"Hello. This is Becky, how may I help you?"

"It's Nicky. You called?"

"Yeah, can you hang on a minute?" Nicky could hear Becky's office door close. "Okay, about Professor Marks. He dropped you from the mentorship. He took on a sophomore with fewer credits total than you had last year. What happened between the two of you?" Becky was whispering.

"Look, I'm glad you let me know." Nicky wasn't glad about anything, but no one could know what she knew. It was her leverage.

"I was asked to call you. I'm supposed to tell you to bring your key to the registrar by next Tuesday or they'll hold your grades."

Now Nicky was mad. She didn't do well with threats.

"I'm sorry." Becky was still talking, as if one-sided conversations were completely acceptable. "I thought you should know the temps are speculating that the two of you had an affair. If Mrs. Marks catches wind…"

"Becky! Please! Am I someone who would have time for an affair? Don't they have anything to do but gossip over there? It's ridiculous! He'll get his stupid key in the morning."

"Yeah, okay. I just wanted to warn you." Becky spoke louder now, obviously sensing a wall going up between them.

When they hung up, Nicky took out her frustration on the mysterious letter in her hand. She jabbed her thumbnail into the side and sliced it across the top in a long, jagged tear.

The game is over, doll. You'll get your A. Just keep your mouth shut!

It wasn't signed. It didn't need to be. Professor Marks had a secret—probably more than one.

When she started working in his office it was with the goal of earning a place on his mentorship team the following year. She answered phones and took messages and copied lecture notes for students. Innocent stuff. She admired his work; that was all. That's how it began.

Things began to unravel the day she brought him a hot chocolate from the student union. She didn't usually do things like that for people, but she wanted him to choose her when the year was up. She wanted to stand out. It wasn't about him really.

He stayed in the office with her that afternoon, and for some reason she was drawn to watching him sip his drink. That was when she saw what all the female students and faculty had droned on about in the ladies' room. He was beautiful. Married, but beautiful.

The flirtation began when she started wearing make-up again. That's when he started grading papers in his office instead of at home while his wife watched HGTV. He wanted to spend the day in his office soaking up Nicky's perfume.

They played their cat-and-mouse game for almost three weeks before the first kiss. Was it an affair? He was married, and they had kissed. It had all been stupid, really. It shouldn't count.

She entertained fantasies about him. She always had a habit of wanting what she couldn't have; not for the chase, but to challenge the boundary. She could feel womanly experiencing feelings for the opposite sex without having to involve herself fully or lose herself in the relationship. She could want a man and not need him. It was safe.

She had been waiting at the printer for the class notes to come through so she could copy them. She stood with her back to the door with her weight on her right foot and her left hand on her hip. She'd spun around quickly, and he was waiting, lips ready, pressed against hers before she could even think. She kissed back—only slightly. A nervous and wary kiss. Then she grabbed the class notes from the machine and left the office, leaving him standing alone, silent and bewildered.

They never talked about that day. She tried to play it off, forgetting it for the sake of his ego—and for the sake of the mentorship. But he began to grade her harshly. It wasn't even subtle. She could have painted her entire apartment with the red ink he used to mark up her papers. He began cutting her down in front of the class. It was as if he loathed her.

Midterms were approaching, and she needed to do well in order to stay in the running for the mentorship program. She decided to print out all the past class notes and review them since she had access to them.

He hadn't been in the office, but his computer had been left on. The fishbowl screensaver was making ocean noises through the speakers, and the gurgling quit when she rested her hand on the mouse. It was an e-mail. She shouldn't have read it, but she did, and in a self-protective move, she even printed it off.

She welcomed the break from him. The tension between them was mountainous, and she needed to get away.

After the talk with Becky, she ate an entire bag of potato chips and drank four glasses of orange soda—her comfort food.

The letter was still there the next morning, staring at her hatefully from the countertop. She had seen it in her sleep, and her morning shower couldn't wash it from her mind. She dressed and took Daryl her mailbox key before driving out of the way to go by the university on her way to the airport. The registrar's office wasn't open this early, so she let herself into his office one last time and placed the key with a note on his desk. Then she locked the door and left campus, heading back to the airport.

The note said enough. She was pleased with it. She hated men who used intimidation to get what they wanted. She was reasonable and didn't need coercion. She wouldn't think about it anymore. It was done, and she was free of him for at least three days.

She arrived at the airport one hour prior to takeoff—just as she'd been advised. Everything was on schedule.

The ticket agent took her boarding pass and she walked through the carpeted tunnel into the plane. The plane wasn't very full when she'd been bumped to first class. She smiled at her luck. Things were surely getting better.

Chapter Two

⁓⁂◎

SIDNEY WAS LOOKING out the window when the flight attendant appeared in the aisle, a young woman behind her.

The young woman took the aisle seat.

Sidney was thankful for her window seat; she always sat by the window when she flew. Watching the clouds was her favorite part of flying—that and peanuts.

Just to be safe, she purchased her own bag of peanuts in the airport lobby. She held the bag of peanuts in her hand, just waiting for the plane to take off so she could justify opening it. She loved to tease herself this way. She did the same thing when she went to the movies. She held a popcorn kernel to her lips through seventeen minutes of previews.

Then, letting it inside, she would soak the salt into her tongue. It pleased her to wait—or it used to. Lately it had felt more like torment than teasing. She had been craving peanuts since she learned she would be flying. Now, with the peanuts in her hand, she imagined the little person inside her impatiently waiting, demanding peanuts.

The young woman beside her was sitting with her head back and her eyes closed. She might as well go ahead and eat the peanuts. There was nothing else to do until she could turn on her laptop.

Thick, white salt crystals littered her lap as she opened the bag. She put a handful of peanuts in her mouth and licked her fingers before brushing off her gray, pinstriped suit pants.

No one would guess that Sidney Michelle Flannery was pregnant. She had the kind of body that could mask such a thing. She wasn't the kind of woman who needed a positive pregnancy test to grow breasts; hers had been there since sixth grade. She had never been fat, and no one would call her chubby; she was solid. Some might say she was big-boned. She saw that as a good thing. She wondered—does the baby have big bones?

She thought about the baby more and more lately. She was obsessed with its gender. She wondered if it would resemble its father. Would people find out?

So far, she'd been successful in her plan. There was no question that it was a brilliant plan. Everyone who knew her knew how much she had always wanted a baby. She craved a baby the way she now craved peanuts. No one had met a boyfriend, and she didn't seem to have any prospects. The baby might have been hard to explain if her plan hadn't been so perfect. Telling them she'd been inseminated wouldn't even seem farfetched.

Nonetheless, her mother worried. After all, Sidney would be turning thirty this year. Hadn't she heard that pregnancies could be complicated around that age?

Mrs. Flannery had called almost every day since she learned Sidney was pregnant. Last Friday Sidney's dad had called her at work and begged her to come home for a visit.

"You know how your mother is. She just needs to get a good look at you, inspect her young, make sure the wee one's not causing you any problems." He was pulling out the big guns, heaping on the guilt.

"Dad, I'm fine. I already told her I'm fine," Sidney had protested.

"I know. I know. But you want your daddy to get some sleep don't you? To tell the truth, I don't think your mother has so much as blinked since you told her!"

"Okay, I'll see about some time off. How are you doing with all this?" She winced the second she asked.

"Oh, honey, as long as it's part of you, I'll love it. You know I will, but…"

"That's it. I knew there'd be a 'but.'"

"Well, it's just that I always thought I was a good daddy. I loved your mom to death. Still do. I can't see why you'd give up on finding that kind of love for yourself. The baby is going to need a daddy, not just a reference number. Anyway, we'll talk when you get here."

It wasn't easy lying to her dad. She ached to tell him the truth. She had found love, but not the kind of love he would ever understand. She wasn't sure she understood it.

She was feeling nauseous just thinking about it. Who knew that hot flashes could come with pregnancy as well as menopause? She unbuttoned her jacket and removed it to reveal the pink shell underneath. They were in the air now, and the use of electronics was approved. She struggled with the seat restraint to reach the laptop case at her feet. With one last look at the woman next to her, she lifted the case, lowered the seatback tray in front of her, and opened her computer.

With a few taps they found each other. He seemed to be waiting—as she had been. They chatted awhile as if they hadn't talked in days. It always felt like that when they were apart.

She didn't know why she loved him; he wasn't her type at all. She liked simple men. She usually fell for the kind of man who read the paper every morning with a cup of coffee. She liked men who solved their own problems, mowed their own lawns, fixed their own cars. She didn't know if he did anything for himself. It wasn't that he wasn't smart. He was very smart. It's just that he had put himself above the simple stuff. There were people he could hire to do things for him, so he wasn't about to be bothered with it.

They had met a year ago at a cocktail party. She'd been dressed to kill. She didn't know he was married until their fifth date. She might never have known if it hadn't been for the envelope addressed to Mr. and Mrs. she found in his glove compartment the night he took her to the opera.

She opened the compartment to hide her cigarettes in it, the way she did in her own car. She might have overlooked it if she hadn't noticed the look on his face. He had the look of a man in trouble.

She should have demanded he take her home the minute he told her.

Unfortunately, Sidney never did what she should do. Instead, she let him fill her with excuses and half-truths—promising his marriage was over and that it had been for years. Something about the way he said it made it feel real, and she let herself love him. It was a sick irony that the doctor claimed it was that night that the baby was conceived.

She knew that decent women would hate her for having an affair with a married man. She'd been disloyal to all females—a traitor of sorts. She knew that no other female would believe her explanation that he loved her more than he had ever loved any woman. And he meant it—in his own way. Didn't he?

She had kept the pregnancy to herself until the first ultrasound, then she scanned the picture and e-mailed it to him with a note that said, *I think he has your eyes. His momma needs to see you tonight. If you can get away, meet me at Henry's around nine.*

She hadn't known if it was a boy, but the prospect of a son always seemed to wake men up. The thought of a junior would be a draw, so she toyed with the possibility.

He hadn't come to Henry's, but he called her cell phone and told her to go back to her apartment because he had a surprise for her.

She arrived to find her apartment filled with blue and pink balloons. He waited for her on the couch as she sifted through them. He seemed happy, but she wanted a guarantee and he couldn't give her one. That's when she decided she wouldn't risk the humiliation. She would deny him as he was denying her. To anyone who asked, her baby was the product of an anonymous donor. She'd even made up an identification number for kicks.

She would make herself look like an independent woman, even though she was bound to a man who would never put her first.

Daddy was waiting outside the airport in his truck. They didn't allow people at the gate anymore, and she was sorry there was no joyous reunion of walking out of the runway and into the arms of family eager to embrace her and rub their hands over her stomach, to carry her luggage.

She paid a dollar for a cart to push her bags to the drive-up pick-up. Daddy didn't even get out of the car. A young airport worker shoved her bag into the extended cab and wandered off with her empty cart. Daddy smiled at her, but that was all. Mom had stayed at home; she had cookies in the oven.

If she hadn't been nervous at the prospect of coming home and facing the task of convincing her mom she was going to be a perfect single mom, she was feeling it as they turned onto Cedar Avenue. Even from the street she could recognize Jon's car. Who had thought to invite her old flame?

With a look at her dad, she knew who was behind it.

"Your baby needs a daddy," he said. Now he was gloating.

The peanuts rumbled in Sidney's stomach, and before she could give warning, she threw up.

Coming home was a mistake.

Chapter Three

JENNIFER WAS FOURTEEN when Nicky and her family moved away. Before that, she couldn't imagine spending a day apart from her best friend. They were the kind of friends that stay so connected it's hard to tell where one ends and the other begins. Even now, as different as they'd become, it was a treat to see each other.

Jennifer's dad had her convinced she was a princess. He had told her that so much that she'd grown to believe it. She had scrupulous taste in men, expensive taste in clothing, and a very determined walk—the walk of a princess, a dancer. Toe before heal, graceful, begging to be applauded.

Nicky and Jennifer had taken ballet together as children. They danced together for hours, wrapped in spandex and tulle.

Then Bradley Frank moved to town, and Nicky traded her ballet shoes for cleats. It was all about boys.

Nicky was the experienced one. Jennifer had always felt like a baby when she listened to Nicky brag about what Brad had said to her or how his breath had tasted. She was sure that she had heard about every encounter her friend had ever had with the opposite sex. She felt immature and childish, certain she would never be kissed. Boys didn't take her seriously. Or maybe they took her too seriously. After all, she was a princess.

Jennifer smiled as she twisted the ring on her finger, making certain the diamond shimmered proudly. Who would ever think that she'd be married first? She loved the accomplishment, how things had changed. Her marriage was happy too, very happy in fact. She had married a prince. Bradley had become quite a man!

It had been a little weird when she first started dating him. Nicky had approved, of course. She had moved away by then and had crushes on about five different guys in the town she had moved to. Bradley had long since been erased from her thoughts. She was no longer interested in him at all.

Nicky had even been the maid of honor at Jennifer and Bradley's wedding. It was a beautiful affair—three hundred people invited, and though she knew there hadn't been that many actually in attendance, the long list made her feel loved.

She wore a princess dress and, of course, a tiara. It was a black-and-white wedding, the height of sophistication. The attendants in her wedding party carried bouquets of herbs—sage, rosemary, and myrtle—rather than traditional flowers. The herbs filled the church with a clean, earthy scent, a subtle way for Bradley to incorporate his first love into their big day.

Bradley was a chef. That's what he said when anyone asked about his job. He always left out the fact that he owned his own restaurant. He had bought the space with money from an inheritance, and he and Jennifer had transformed it into a premier dining establishment.

Jennifer still danced. As a matter of fact, she taught dance now. Her life was just as she had dreamed it would be. Well, almost.

It had been exactly three months since the doctor had given her the news that she and Bradley would never conceive by natural means. She would never have a child, genetically speaking. They had immediately thought of the same solution, but Bradley was too much of a gentleman to broach the subject. They both knew what they needed to do, but he wouldn't push.

It had taken two months to get the nerve to make the phone call, and still she couldn't tell her best friend exactly why she needed her to come for a visit. They had to talk this through in person. Jennifer was a princess, but she'd never been selfish. It was a lot to ask, and she knew it. She would give choices, be flexible. Nicky liked to feel in charge. All that mattered was that there would be a baby.

She would leave it to Nicky to choose between carrying the baby or donating an egg for another woman to carry. Jennifer had her preference. She knew she could trust Nicky to carry her baby and to include her in the process. However, Jennifer knew it would be a stretch for her best friend.

Jennifer had dreamed of a baby with her nose and Brad's smile, a perfect blend of their love. Now she would dream of a child who resembled her and prayed that Nicky would birth it.

She couldn't imagine Nicky pregnant. Even to think of it was hilarious. She could picture Nicky cussing out the bump when it made her designer jeans impossible to wear. She'd spend nine months on bed rest, treating pregnancy as if it were a terminal disease. The baby would be born with acne from all the junk food Nicky would consume. He or she would be addicted to orange soda before birth.

Nicky would choose to donate an egg and be done with it. She was almost sure.

It didn't matter. No one would know the difference. People always assumed they were sisters anyway. They had always resembled one another. Even their baby pictures looked alike.

It was bad timing, and Jennifer knew it. Nicky was fast approaching a mentorship that had been the focus of her entire college career. She couldn't stop now.

Jennifer looked in the rearview mirror and ruffled her hair with her hands. It had a tendency to look flat despite its thickness. She applied a thin layer of clear gloss to her lips, took a deep breath, and opened the car door. The line at the drive-up was insane; she decided it was worth a parking fee to be out of the mess of travelers.

She could see Nicky waiting on a bench and checking her watch. They spotted each other, and Jennifer felt her heart thump.

Jennifer had a sudden flash of memory of a summer when they were young—she would guess they were around twelve—and they both had wanted dogs. Both sets of parents turned down their requests. They had been desperate for a pet. It all seemed silly now, how they had filled their desire by buying Sparky. Sparky was a goldfish they bought together at

Mr. Finn's Fish Shoppe. They split the cost of his bowl and food, and Sparky rotated back and forth between homes every month.

It was the fourth rotation when Jennifer found Sparky floating at the top of his bowl. The fish hadn't been eating the flakes she'd given him. She fed him each morning as she got ready for school. First she tried giving the fish worms—it worked for fishing, she reasoned. Days passed, and her concern grew. In a desperate attempt to get him to eat she put a scoop of ice cream in the fishbowl.

Sparky didn't last very long in the mushy mix of water, worms, and vanilla ice cream.

Nicky didn't speak to her for a week. Jennifer wondered what she would think now. Would she remember Sparky and decide Jennifer was too dumb to mother a child?

"How was the flight?" Jennifer asked as they walked back to the car.

"Slept most of it. What's the plan?" Nicky answered.

Nicky looked unbelievably good for having just gotten off a plane.

"Well, it's three o'clock now. Let's pick up something to drink. Brad is cooking something up for us. He took the day off, and I have an appointment at six."

Jennifer didn't want to expand on the appointment thing yet. Not before Brad was with her. She couldn't do it alone.

Soon they arrived at the house. Nicky took a shower, while Jennifer sat in the kitchen watching Brad cut up tomatoes for the salad.

"Have you said anything to her yet?" He asked Jennifer as he concentrated on the knife.

"I'm the world's biggest chicken."

"No, you're not."

"I am. Seriously, all I could think of was Sparky."

"That dumb fish you killed? Why?"

"See, that's just it. I killed it. I couldn't even keep a fish alive! Maybe I'm not fit to be a mother. Maybe God knows I'm not and made me this way on purpose."

"Stop it." He had left the tomato and was rubbing her shoulders.

"We are going to have children some day, and you will be an excellent mother. You haven't killed me yet, and look at Georgie. She loves you, gets slobber all over you every chance she gets."

Jennifer was trying not to cry as she watched Georgie, their Yorkie pup, who was sleeping on her tiny bed in the living room.

Brad was kissing his way up her neck when Nicky cleared her throat behind them and snickered.

"Take a longer shower next time," Brad teased.

The table was set with their best dishes, and candles glistened in the center. A salad bowl was filled with rich green lettuce, egg, bacon, and garden tomatoes. Beside it was a plate of bread, and she could see Brad filling three plates with tender steak, potatoes, and peas in Alfredo sauce. It wasn't just a dinner. This was an occasion. There was something to say, some news to tell. There had to be.

"Do you have bad news, or is this about a baby?" Nicky asked.

"Both," Brad answered.

Jennifer watched her plate and played with her peas. It felt like a bad dream, the kind of dream where there are a million things you should say, you want to say, but when you open your mouth nothing comes out. As much as you want to, you cannot. She felt foolish. It was unnatural.

Nicky listened as Brad explained the problems they had conceiving and asked her for something she didn't expect.

She felt powerful, and for once, her power felt all wrong.

Chapter Four

THE RICH FLAVOR and warm aroma of Mom's cookies would have been a welcome delight normally. But Sidney couldn't get past the acidic taste of the peanuts that had made her sick.

"Oh my!" was all Mom said when she saw her. But that was enough to shatter Sidney's confidence and confirm her belief that she was a mess.

She took a shower in the basement bathroom, where the pressure was stronger. Dad had installed a special new showerhead a few years ago, and the hot water felt wonderful as it pelted her neck.

She washed her hair, stepped out of the shower, and wrapped herself in an Egyptian cotton towel. It felt good to be home.

The loose sundress she put on had been purchased pre-pregnancy, but it took on a different look now. Her new body stretched and pulled the fabric, reshaping it around the tiny bump that looked a bit more like what it really was in the dress.

She slipped on sandals and applied a small amount of lip gloss. Her perfect skin didn't require much make-up. Sometimes she wore thick eye makeup, and when she did she looked like Cleopatra. She could look like the girl next door and manage to look exotic at the same time. She wondered what it was about her that had attracted Peter Marks.

She missed him now. She ached for a normal relationship—the kind of relationship she could tell her parents about. She wanted to eat dinner in public without wondering who might see them together. She wanted to spend the night with him, not work him up and send him home to his beautiful wife.

And there was no doubt, Alexis was beautiful. Sidney had seen her picture in Peter's wallet. She looked artsy, Bohemian. She probably reeked of patchouli; but in her own way, she was beautiful.

Sidney had wondered about how different they were, complete opposites for sure. She decided it was a good thing, proof that Peter's marriage was dead. He wasn't looking for anyone who resembled his wife.

She opened the door and stomped up the stairs.

"You look much better," Mom said as she walked over to feel at the bump. "Does the baby feel better now?"

"Couldn't tell you. He changes his mind on a whim," Sidney answered.

Silverware and dishes were out but hadn't been put on the table yet. She began helping. "What did you make?"

"Well, I tried to think bland for you. What can I say though? I need flavor. I made peppercorn chicken, carrots, and cornbread the way Grandma made it."

Sidney would have gotten sick again had the meal not been redeemed by the cornbread.

Five plates. That meant Jon must be staying for dinner. Mom, Dad, Mitchell, Sidney, and yes… Jon.

It wouldn't be too terrible. She just wouldn't look at him. Never meet him in the eye.

He knew her too well. He'd expose her. Yet she knew how hard it would be to look away. She remembered clearly that he wasn't the type you could look away from easily. He was the type you catch yourself staring at while your mind races to what you will name his children—the type of guy girls fantasize about after dark when they should be sleeping. She had to admit, she would be glad to see him.

It seemed twisted, the way she felt guilty for wanting to see him, as if she were cheating on Peter. Oddly enough, though, she'd never seen Peter look ashamed. In fact, when she thought about it, he actually seemed a little proud of himself.

She heard the back door open and Jon was there. He looked her over, searching her for evidence of the baby inside her.

"I hope you don't mind. Your dad invited me and, well, I thought it would be nice to see you," he said nervously.

"Yeah, sure. You just missed Mom's cooking, didn't you?" She smiled and laughed and they hugged. He helped her set the table and sat down beside her.

"So how far along are you?"

"Only three and a half months," she answered.

She heard Mitchell snicker in the living room.

"I didn't know they counted by halves," Mitchell teased.

"Actually, smart mouth, they count by weeks. This just sounds shorter. It keeps me in single digits this way."

"We told him how you conceived," Mom added.

Sidney could feel her face get hot. Great! Jon, perfect Jon, knew that she had claimed artificial insemination. She felt like a child caught in a lie, though no one knew at all.

It was one thing for Mom and Dad and Mitchell to believe her. Jon should know better. Shouldn't he?

They had talked about having children several times back when they were in love—back when it was cool to have long hair, short skirts, and big dreams. That was before rap music talked politics and Madonna was a mom. It had been a while, but she remembered. She told him about her dream of her son catching his first fish with his dad—Jon maybe. She could picture a little girl with pigtails riding on her daddy's shoulders the way she had when she was a child. Her dreams had included a daddy for her children and a man—a husband—to hold her at night. She wondered if Jon remembered those talks.

After dinner Mitchell began fussing in front of the mirror as he got ready for a date with a girl he had met at a friend's hockey game. Mom and Dad began getting ready to leave as well. It seemed they had obligated themselves to attend the Morgans' anniversary party. They had responded months ago, they said, before they knew she was coming. It wouldn't be polite to say they were coming and then not show up or cancel at the last minute. Surely she understood.

She had, for the most part, understood that their lives continued whether she was visiting or not. However, she did feel a bit like an outsider as she watched them hustle about the house.

"What will you do while we're out?" Mom asked.

"Don't worry about me," she answered, trying not to look at Jon. She could feel him watching her.

"I'll keep her busy," Jon answered.

It hadn't truly been a set-up; but it absolutely felt like one.

"Is it okay if I use the phone to make a long-distance call?" Sidney asked her dad.

"Sure," he answered. "We'll be home early."

Jon waited for her on the couch while she saw her family out the door, then went into the other room to use the phone.

She checked her watch. He should be alone by now. Alexis had pottery class every Saturday at this time.

"Hello?" It was a woman answering. "Hello?"

It was Alexis.

"Hello. Is Mr. Marks available?" Sidney couldn't believe she was bold enough to ask. She wondered if she was being bold or stupid.

"Who is this?"

"Umm... I'm in Professor Marks' class." How stupid! Classes had ended; they're done. He had no classes until the end of next month.

"I should have known you would call here," Sidney could hear the shakiness in Alexis' voice. Her voice was gentle though—even fragile—in her anger. "You're bold enough to ask for my husband. Be bold enough to say your name, Sidney. I know it. I know who you are. I know that you drink too much at cocktail parties. I know you drive a white car with a sunroof. I know that you have a passion for pink lingerie. I know that.

"I also know you are carrying a baby that you claim is Peter's. There is something else I know, Sidney. Something I'm sure you know too. Peter doesn't love me, maybe he never will, but he doesn't love you either. Peter loves Peter, and that's all. He'll never leave me. He'd lose everything. Peter isn't home tonight, but he isn't with you either, apparently. I can promise you this though, Sidney. Peter isn't alone."

Sidney couldn't speak. Alexis' voice was breaking and she was beginning to cry when she hung up.

Suddenly Sidney felt like a traitor—a traitor to women, specifically Alexis. It was strange how she'd regarded her before tonight. She'd imagined a cold, emotionless, loveless, clueless woman. She pictured her as someone undeserving of love and romance from Peter or from anyone. But the voice she heard was the voice of a woman who was emotional, soft, and tired of loving and not receiving love in return. Maybe she deserved love after all. Maybe she had earned it with constant hurt and dwindling pride. Maybe Sidney had stolen it from her. Sidney also felt like a traitor to the child inside her. She could imagine the baby's anger. Was the baby angry because there was little chance he or she would ever know a father's love? Peter would never carry a child on his shoulders, and she knew that. But now she was forced to ask herself, *Will they ever meet? Am I fooling myself?*

Her stomach began to hurt. *Really* hurt.

Chapter Five

ALEXIS HAD A lot of stories she could tell about Peter, but probably no one would believe them. The Peter she knew and loved had pretty much ceased to exist years ago. He was a different man now—someone she didn't like much. She was still in love with her memories of him though, and she'd be faithful to him until the day she died.

They had met in art school. Probably the first thing people would be surprised to know about Peter was that he had gone to art school. He used to draw with charcoals. He blended the thick, black sticks with his thumb or pinky finger. She could still remember the smudges he'd get on his cheek when he pushed back his hair, or on his lips when he bit his fingernails. He used to tell her he loved her.

Two years into their marriage, she had become pregnant. She cherished every second of her nine months before delivering Zeek, her beautiful angel baby. His name was Zachary, but they had shortened it to Zeek. They both loved the name Zachary, but it seemed like too big a name for such a tiny person.

People had mostly forgotten about Zeek. He lived for three wonderful and difficult years. They were years filled with doctor appointments and surgeries, hope and tears. He was such a good boy, and Peter had been a good dad. Peter never doubted that Zeek would get better. He believed that somehow all the love he gave him would be enough to heal Zeek's unhealthy heart. He believed they would always be a family.

Zeek loved cars. He called them beep-beeps. He raced them on the kitchen floor as she made dinner, and he carried at least one little toy car with him everywhere he went.

Peter and Zeek washed their family car on weekends, and the soapy water flattened Zeek's hair and made him look like a drowned kitten.

When Zeek went into the hospital the last time he took a toy car with him that he thought looked like his daddy's car.

After Zeek died they moved to a smaller house, and Peter went back to school and eventually became a history professor. He stopped drawing and stopped telling her he loved her.

She had needed him so badly. She wanted him to hold her and encourage her to keep breathing. She was fighting for her life.

Alexis had dedicated her life to Zeek. It seemed as if taking care of him was all she had ever done. After his death she was lost and without direction, and she turned to art. It was familiar, therapeutic, expressive art.

She took a pottery class on Saturdays, watercolor on Mondays, and modern dance on Thursdays. She got a part-time job as an assistant interior designer. She kept busy, stayed numb, and she and Peter grew further and further apart.

No one had to tell her about his first affair; she had just known. He stopped avoiding her and instead tried to pick fights with her. It was as if he wanted her to hate him, was begging her to blame him. He was trying to excuse himself from their marriage.

That's when she became too sweet, too gentle, and too meek, avoiding confrontations at all cost. She would not be his excuse to leave. She would love him, painful as it was, and if he left, he would have only himself to blame.

Alexis didn't know how many women there had been, but she knew enough for any trust she had ever had in womankind to be shattered. She knew enough to suspect every woman she met, and Alexis was very lonely.

She knew she was not entirely blameless; she had almost had an affair herself. She had been asked. It was a younger man in her pottery class. He was very sexy, talented; a young Peter, really.

She had told him no and hadn't gone back to class since. She was, however, flattered. She had to admit that she had even fantasized about him briefly. When she was given the option, though, she said no. Her heart belonged to one man, and it would remain with him, even though it was in pieces.

The first week she missed pottery class she went shopping. She came home early and Peter was still not home. She drove to campus to surprise him, motivated to find the old Peter, the unbroken Peter, and make him look at her the way the young potter had.

She let herself into his office and spun around in his chair a few times, just waiting.

A letter was taped to his computer, and she read it. It was a nosy, sneaky thing to do, but she didn't regret it now.

There was a picture of a fetus and an attached e-mail from a woman named Sidney. There was a second, handwritten message lying underneath the e-mail—a letter scribbled in blue ink that said:

Professor Marks,

You and I both know that this mentorship belonged to me. I earned it so completely. Men like you disgust me. I will never respect you again. You use your power to get your way. I think it's very weak to steal a woman's dream because she won't sleep with you. Or because she knows who has. My own pride kept me from reporting you to the dean. My pity kept me from speaking to your wife. It was a call I very much wanted to make. I didn't make it, and I won't, because I, unlike you, do not enjoy hurting people and wrecking their futures. However, be sure that I will not hesitate to report you to the police if I ever—and I do mean ever—receive another threatening letter from you. I may want a career like yours someday, but I do not wish to be you.

Nicky Bell
P.S. God help your child!

Alexis recognized the name instantly. Nicky Bell was Peter's assistant. She had always seemed very efficient and always relayed the messages she left for Peter very promptly. She had seemed polite on the phone, professional.

The next day Alexis took Becky, the office secretary, to lunch. She pushed and probed, and eventually learned a lot about her husband.

She began reviewing personal financial documents and found a credit card bill for Victoria's Secret. That's when she learned that Sidney liked pink. She learned about the white car from a neighbor. She had known enough, but now she knew too much.

Alexis boiled with anger, and all the emotions she had stuffed down and ignored since Zeek died began to surface. They had lost their baby, and here was Peter, making a new baby with some bimbo on the side. She was raw.

Every time he looked at her she wanted to spit in his face. Every time she felt him touch her, she had a burning desire to tear off whatever flesh he had touched.

It was a week of anger, tears, and silence, and Peter hadn't even noticed.

Alexis was glad when she got the call from Sidney—glad for the confrontation. It made her feel like a woman—strong, centered, and unrelenting. She was not going down without a fight. She was not going to be permissive and pretend to be naïve. She deserved better. She would not let this woman steal her husband or her life. She had lost one love—her poor, innocent Zeek. She would not be alone.

The door opened as she hung up the phone, and she didn't even try to hide her tears. She was shaking and sobbing, and for a moment Peter felt something.

"I wasn't where you think," he said quietly.

"I know. She called for you," Alexis answered.

"Who?"

"Are there that many?" she snapped. "Sidney, the mother of your child. The child that matters."

"What does that mean? You don't think Zeek mattered to me?" She could see that he was offended, but she didn't care. After what he'd done he didn't have the right to be angry.

"You loved him so much that you hurt his mother every day. You loved him so much that it kills you to even say his name. Is that love, Peter? Do you know what love looks like? Because there's a little more to it than pink lingerie! I know what love looks like. I know all about commitment and heartbreak, and I love anyway. But I'm tired, Peter. I'm tired of loving you when you're in another woman's bed. Having a child! You're having a child with her, Peter!"

He turned his back on her, his eyes swollen. He was angry whether he had the right or not. He had loved Zeek. He'd even loved her. He just hadn't loved himself. He walked out the door, leaving her shaking and vulnerable, not knowing if he would ever return.

First, she cleaned the kitchen. Cleaning eased her stress.

Next, she lit candles and took a long, hot bath. It was a romantic bath that did nothing to calm her and only made her feel angrier.

When she had dried off and slipped into her most comfortable pajamas, she went to the den and logged onto the Internet.

Good, her sister Kristen was on line. She smiled for the first time in hours.

I need to talk, Alexis typed.

I'm listening.

She had just begun to write about Sidney and the baby when her phone rang.

It was Kristen. "Let's use our voices, if you don't mind."

"I just don't know what to do."

"Do something for yourself maybe. Stop waiting for him to take care of you. It isn't happening, and you have to take care of yourself. Do something fun."

"How? This is so huge it's all I can think about," Alexis said.

"I have an idea. I'll call you back," Kristen said. There was an excited edge in her voice.

Half an hour later Alexis' phone rang again.

"Get some sleep. Your flight leaves at 10 AM, American Airlines. It's a coach ticket, though. Is that okay?"

"Fine, but what about Peter?"

"Forget Peter! Leave him a note if you want, but you're coming," Kristen insisted.

There was no arguing with Kristen when her mind was made up. It was a big-sister thing. Kristen wouldn't take no for an answer, and Alexis knew better than to try.

She packed her bag and went to sleep alone, snuggled deep into Peter's pillow.

Chapter Six

FROM THE DAY Nicky arrived she knew this was going to be a longer visit than she had intended.

She worried about the doctor appointment all night long to the point she hardly slept. She wondered if Jennifer had.

Brad had told her about the miscarriages as he explained the whole thing to Nicky prior to their meeting with Dr. Olsander the night before. Nicky couldn't understand how Jennifer had gotten through such a terrible time without telling her. Why had Jennifer not even mentioned it?

Nicky knew it was disgustingly selfish to feel insecure about it. Still, she couldn't help obsess about what such an enormous omission said about the state of their friendship.

The six o'clock meeting with Dr. Olsander helped explain a lot. Jennifer had fibroids in the uterine cavity. Her condition had caused the miscarriages and was the reason she could not conceive. There was a complication with her ovaries that made it necessary to have a donor. They needed eggs, and they were asking for Nicky's. Jennifer liked that their resemblance would make the baby look very much like her own biological child. None of the choices were easy.

Nicky could donate an egg, and a surrogate could carry the baby. But a surrogate was a stranger, and Nicky could understand how vulnerable the surrogate option made Jennifer feel.

The option Jennifer and Brad hoped Nicky would accept was called traditional surrogacy. Nicky would have eggs harvested and fertilized by Brad's sperm then transferred back into her womb for her to carry for nine months.

It seemed strange no matter how she looked at it. They had been sitting in a room discussing Brad's sperm fertilizing her eggs as Jennifer fought to remain strong.

Dr. Olsander was very nice. She was informative and easy to like. She made eye contact with all of them and treated them as equal members in a very big decision.

"We need to be a team if we proceed," she said to all of them.

"The advantage is that you are already friends and trust each other, but this is an emotional process. We all need to communicate with each other."

Nicky had all the facts, and they all agreed to sleep on it. They set an appointment for the next day. It had been a whirlwind. Nicky didn't sleep on it; she stayed awake and paced the floor.

It was a huge decision, a colossal decision. She was being asked to commit her body to housing another life for nine months, knowing she would be left alone in the end.

It was beside the point that Nicky didn't want children of her own. Having a baby and then letting it go seemed unfathomable. Then again, it wouldn't be hers once she signed the agreement papers, even though, biologically, it was hers and would always be hers. Would the child ever know the truth? Nicky hated to think about lying to him or her. Then again, if Nicky didn't want to be a mother anyway, and didn't think of herself that way, would the child need to know?

Nicky couldn't think straight. Pregnancy, surrogacy—these were life-changing words. They were words with big meaning, big commitment, and big risk. It didn't matter how she thought it through—selfishly or not—there was one word that dominated all others—friendship. That loomed over every doubt and fear and gripped her with a certainty she'd never known before. There was really no question then, nothing to decide. For at least nine months, her life belonged to her friend. In the end, Nicky would give the gift of motherhood.

It was somewhere around three o'clock in the morning when Nicky finally slid under the covers. It was the perfect place to dream. Fluffy pillows nestled her face; warm, soft, yellow sheets that smelled like lemons caressed her. Leave it to Jennifer to think of every detail.

Love is in the details. Nicky had heard that somewhere—probably from Oprah. Love meant going above and beyond. It was then that she realized how much she loved Brad and Jennifer as if they were family. More than her family if she was truthful. They were her family, and she was going to give them a family of their own.

She was glad for a moment, before all conscious thought ceased. She was glad that her life hadn't gone entirely her way, glad for the curve in the road and the mysterious unknown that lay before her. It was an adventure. She was on the verge of something great.

There was a click-clack noise that broke her slumber at nine o'clock. It was Jennifer, pulling back the drapes. If the noise hadn't woke her, the streaming rays of sunshine would have. Jennifer couldn't wait another moment. She needed to know where her life was headed. She needed to know if Nicky was going to be her heroine or just remain her best friend. In either case, Jennifer needed to talk.

The bedsprings bounced a little as she sat on the end of the bed.

"Good morning," she chirped hopefully.

"Are you serious?" Nicky groaned.

"Come on! Get up. I want to spend some time with you," Jennifer coaxed.

"Are you sure you aren't my mother?" Nicky teased, rubbing her eyes with her fists.

"Up, up, up, and at 'em!" Jennifer laughed, trying her best impression of Mrs. Bell.

Nicky rested her head on her hands and leaned up on her elbows, forcing herself to accept that it was day.

"We don't have to discuss your decision yet if you haven't made one, but if you have, spare me, because my nerves are shot. I just have to know something."

"Well," Nicky began, watching her friend's eyes drop. "I need to talk to you about this. I've got some questions."

"Sure."

"Just listen. I'm your best friend, right? I mean, after Brad, of course."

Jennifer nodded.

"How could you not tell me what you've been through? Miscarriages aren't nothing. It had to be horrible for you, and you didn't say a word about it. Don't you trust me?"

Jennifer was deliberately avoiding eye contact. If their eyes met there would be tears, and it was too early in the day to have a meltdown.

"I guess I didn't want it to be real, like if no one knew then it didn't really happen. It's not you; I mean I haven't really talked to Brad, either. I will when I'm ready. It's just hard."

"Okay. I understand. As long as you know that I'm here when you're ready. I need you to promise to be real with me and share what you're feeling over the next nine months. Maybe you can go through tough times alone, but I can't. I'm going to need you. We've got to do it together, okay?"

Jennifer's head raised and a smile spread across her face. "You're going to do it?"

"Yup. You're going to be a momma, Mrs. Frank, if I can do anything about it."

That's when reserved, polite, rational Jennifer disappeared and a giddy schoolgirl replaced her. She jumped up and down on the lemon-scented sheets and squealed like a teenager.

"I'm going to be a mommy!" she screamed.

Chapter Seven

THE DAY WAS theirs. It was a day marked forever by the decisions that were made. They had a bond strong enough to see beyond loss, beyond secrets, beyond time.

It was strange how much they had let Peter control their relationship. It was subtle, like a dance. Like one of the old dances where you begin with one partner and are slowly passed to others so casually that by the end of the song you can't remember your original partner.

Alexis and Kristen had moved apart slowly, both physically and emotionally. It was important to regain some lost ground, it was meaningful for Alexis to take back a piece of herself she'd let Peter control.

Peter felt threatened by Kristen. He probably had good reason. Sisters talk, and it was no secret what Kristen thought of him.

It wasn't anything specific at first, just the tone of voice on the phone that told Kristen that Alexis wasn't happy. Sure, she had a lot building up inside; Zeek's death swallowed her heart whole, making her raw. There was something deeper though, loneliness that was almost audible. She shouldn't have been lonely. He shouldn't have let her be alone, quiet, and thoughtful. It was too dangerous. There was a lot that Peter shouldn't have done.

It didn't matter now. Kristen wanted to believe that one day of mind-blowing fun could erase hours, days, weeks, and years of her sister's emotional pain. She was simple that way. She was matter-of-fact. Things would get better simply because she believed they could. Thinking it was enough to make it so. She was idealistic and cheery to a fault. Kristen was a nurse, and it was her job to make people feel better. There was nothing she couldn't fix.

The glorious day of sisterly bonding began the moment Alexis woke up. It wasn't exactly early. When Alexis couldn't cry anymore the day before, her body surrendered and her mind freed her at last to dream the rest of the day away.

Alexis took a steamy shower and dried off in a fluffy tan robe. She rolled the pomade in her hand and massaged it slowly through her damp hair, trying hard to appear put together. She brushed her teeth and remembered Peter and his love of the scent and taste of cinnamon. She could hear him misting cinnamon breath spray on his tongue, and she remembered the taste of it on his lips when he kissed her good-bye each morning. Had he done it for her, or had it been something to impress the ladies? Like peroxide disinfecting a wound, had he meant to remove any trace of her from his mouth? Had it been to erase her? In that moment she hated cinnamon—the taste, the smell, even the color red. Especially the color red. Her anger was building, and she spit the toothpaste out in disgust just as the bathroom door opened.

"Goodness! I can try another flavor. Is it that gross?" Kristen asked.

Alexis shook her head.

"Don't worry too much how you look. I booked us for massages, and with the oils they use you'll want to shower afterwards."

Alexis dropped her robe and pulled on her velour, JLo-inspired sweats. No, they weren't called sweats anymore. What were they? They were certainly more fashionable than sweats.

"Wow! When did you get curves?" Kristen asked, eyes wide.

"They aren't curves. They're Godiva and Snyder's pretzels."

"No, that's not fat! I know fat when I see fat. It can't be the pretzels. There's nothing in pretzels, and Snyder's are fat free. No, you've got curves, girl. Thirty-two, and you've finally got 'em!"

Alexis laughed and zipped up her top.

Kristen brushed her long hair into a ponytail and pushed it into a claw clip so it cascaded up and down in a young and hip style.

It seemed so strange to them that they both looked like women. It was strange having to think about age when they bought clothes. They weren't old or anything, they just weren't in high school either. They were at a point where life was life, good or bad. Things were real and practical. There was no place in their closets for pink mohair or silver pleather pants. They were in the land of cotton, maybe cashmere, and fleece—lots of fleece. They lived in Sketchers and dreamed of stilettos. They were not "Sex in the City," and they wondered if anyone really was.

A thin blonde swished over to them and offered something to drink. "Spring water? Hot tea? A glass of wine?" She seemed to whisper the words with her hands held close to her face like a teacher talks to a kindergarten class.

Kristen accepted the offer of spring water and gave her sister a disapproving glance when she requested the wine. The blonde had turned to get the drinks before Alexis could change her mind. It was okay. She really did want the wine. She drank infrequently as it was, it would be a treat upon a treat. Peter couldn't drink wine. All of his mistakes were made with good old domestic beer, always in a glass with ice. He was allergic to red wine. His throat swelled and his voice went hoarse. White wine gave him migraines.

She drank red wine that was thick and fruity. She soaked up the smell and swished the sweetness through her teeth. She was feeling sophisticated.

Before long they were greeted by two female masseuses. They were taken to different rooms with lockers where they put on warm, white, terrycloth robes and black, rubber flip-flops.

The robe felt like sixty pounds of warm fabric on Alexis' shoulders, and it had pockets that were lined with soft, black satin, soothing her hands.

She looked in the tiny dressing room mirror, half expecting to see the sophisticated, confident woman she felt like at that moment. She was saddened by the tired, broken face staring back.

Kristen knocked on the dressing room door. "They're ready. We can go in now."

"I'm coming." Alexis removed her necklace and shoved it into the silky black pocket.

From the medium length chain hung a white-gold pendant of a pregnant body. Alexis found the unique pendant in an antique shop when she was pregnant with Zeek. The necklace had a very ancient-looking and eternal warmth to it, like the very practice of motherhood. Peter knew she simply had to have the primal symbol of what she would forever be. He had given it to her during her second trimester, when her belly looked rather like the one on the pendant. He presented it to her in their bedroom, comparing her to the pendant.

There was love then, unquestioned and passionate. They were friends and lovers and parents. Now they were empty and alone.

Alexis followed Kristen into the massage room. The two tables ran parallel to each other, draped with linens soft enough to sooth. The lights were dim burnt-orange, like the flame of a candle just out of sight.

Music was soft and echoed through the room. A sound machine made dripping watery noises that made it seem as if they were in a dank cavern, somewhere exotic and humid.

Alexis removed her robe, climbed on the table, and slid under the sheets. Soon warm fingers were pressing into her back as a toddler presses into Play-Doh. She could hear Kristen moan, and she laughed a little.

There wasn't much talking in the room. They were both melting from sensory overload, letting knots surface and be kneaded out—talking to themselves on the inside.

Kristen was mentally rearranging her house to make room for Alexis, picturing the space crowded up with her potter's wheel. Would she be willing to part with it, for a while at least? Would it even be fair to ask? What about the bookcase? Alexis would get it in the divorce, if there was a divorce. Kristen had always wanted the bookcase. She never really understood how Alexis had come to have it in the first place.

As the oldest, it should have been offered to Kristen first. It would look perfectly at home in her living room beside the green reading chair, next to the fire.

Would Alexis go to church with her? Her sister had always found excuses before for why she couldn't go. Given the circumstances, it seemed almost impossible to avoid it. The singles program would be excellent for Alexis. Kristen had found such comfort from the group just from knowing she wasn't the only single thirty-four-year-old-woman on the planet. God must have something wonderful for her out there somewhere.

What would God say about all this? He would know that Peter is… well… Peter. Peter wasn't capable of caring for a puppy, much less an emotional, vulnerable, spirited woman like Alexis. He was too self-centered to be a husband. God must know this. Peter was controlling and abusive to Alexis' emotions. Surely that wasn't okay. Would Peter give her a divorce? He liked things on his terms. His ego would burn at the thought of someone divorcing, leaving, and rejecting him.

Kirsten laughed at the picture in her mind. She felt almost guilty for disliking him so much. It wasn't right, and she knew better. God could restore anything, even Peter, if He wished. She should pray for him.

Alexis was thinking about clay, pottery class, and the man she had rejected. He had massive hands and muscles that tightened his sleeves when he worked. He was sexy at work. He slid his hands over the clay so forcefully, pressing into it then smearing it on his forehead as he brushed away a curl. She wanted to be the clay, caressed in his warm hands. How different things would be now if she had gone home with him.

Then Peter would be the fool rather than her. Peter would be lonely and homeless, not her.

Would Peter let that woman stay in their house now? Would she sleep in their bed? Would they make love under the handmade quilt her grandma had made and given them as a wedding present? She could picture the other woman in maternity clothes, then cradling a baby that should have been hers and laying it down in Zeek's cradle.

No, Peter wouldn't be that mean. He couldn't. He wouldn't, would he? She had to get Zeek's things in the divorce. Oh God, divorce? Has it come to that? Who would file? Did it have to be her? What if? Would she ever see him again? Would it be as if she had buried him too?

Then she realized that she had been missing Peter—*her* Peter—for a long time. Longer than she could say.

"Try to relax," the masseuse whispered.

Try to relax, she told herself.

She knew she had to go home, face him again, even if it was just to say good-bye. Not today, of course. But eventually, she would have to go home.

Chapter Eight

SIDNEY TRIED TO ignore the pain at first. She wiped her face with her hand and returned to the living room, where Jon patiently waited.

He turned and looked at her. Knowing her as he did, he must know something was very wrong. "Why don't you lie down? You look pale. Are you okay?" He asked, trying to soothe her.

"I'm okay." But she was scared, angry, and feeling alone and unlovable. And she was in physical pain that took her breath away.

"You are *not* okay. What's wrong? Tell me so I can help." He was becoming irritated. "Is it the baby?"

She began to cry. "I'm not sure. It just hurts." She held her stomach.

Jon grabbed his cell phone with one hand and took her arm with the other. He dialed Mr. Morgan's cell phone and was speaking to Sidney's dad before she could object. He was steering her toward his car, letting go of her only long enough to shut the door behind them.

It was dark on Cedar Avenue as Jon headed north toward the Corbin Bridge Health Clinic.

"Are you okay?" he asked, holding her hand briefly before shifting gears.

"I'm scared," she whispered.

"I know. Your parents said they'd meet us there, but I'm going to stay with you until they come. I won't leave you. Unless you want me to." He looked at her. "Look, I know we have a complicated past, but we're still friends, right?"

"Yes," Sidney answered. She needed a friend—someone she could be truthful with. But she wasn't sure if Jon was that person.

The car turned into the hospital parking lot and Jon quickly parked in the only available spot near the entrance. Together they entered the hospital through the revolving doors. He pushed against the glass as Sidney shuffled beside him holding her stomach.

Inside, the waiting room was nearly empty. A drunk was holding ice on his right hand, which was wrapped in a dishtowel. There was also a little boy with his mom. He was crying hard, and a trail of snot slid out of one nostril. It touched his lip for a second before he licked it away and took a breath. He had stuck a marble up his nose and couldn't get it out. His nostril was red and swollen. Sidney remembered when Mitchell had done the same thing with a raisin. Mom had put a straw up his nose and sucked the raisin out. She wondered if that would work with a marble.

A nurse in pink scrubs came to get Sidney and Jon and led them back to a room. She set down her clipboard and hooked Sidney up to a fetal monitor. She was under a sheet with her dress pulled up. Even though she was covered except for her stomach, she felt uncomfortable with Jon there. He sat in the corner in an armchair.

Before long a cart was wheeled into the room and a kindly nurse named Donna began to squeeze blue gel over Sidney's stomach. Sidney craned her neck to watch the computer screen as Donna began the ultrasound. The nurse lingered in one spot for a while and Sidney tried not to wince at the awkward pressure of the medical wand against her stomach. Donna seemed to be trying to get views of the same spot from different angles. Occasionally she would put marks around an area that caught her attention.

"Does the father have heart problems?" the nurse finally asked.

"She doesn't know." Jon began to explain the insemination story.

Sidney stopped him. "Yes."

They both looked at her.

"Well, he doesn't exactly, but there are heart problems in his family."

Suddenly she thought of Zeek. Oh God, why hadn't she thought of it before? "His son died from heart complications."

"How old was he?" The nurse asked.

"Two or three. Two, I think."

Jon was eyeing her, looking confused.

"Should we call him?" Jon asked, insinuating something.

"No, not until we know something."

The nurse wrote something on the printout and stared at the monitor. She appeared to have found something of concern, but she was following protocol and said nothing.

When the doctor came in at last he reviewed the nurse's notes with intensity. He examined Sidney, and he told her he would make an appointment for her with a local doctor who specialized in fertility problems and high-risk pregnancies. He stressed the importance of keeping the appointment.

After scheduling the appointment for two days later the doctor returned to her with a prescription and ordered bed rest until her appointment. He also suggested that she speak to the baby's father to find out more about his son's heart condition. She was to return if there was bleeding.

Mom and Dad arrived, but Jon insisted on driving her home.

"You need to tell them," he said as her parents walked to their car.

"Tell them?" She tried to look naïve.

"Come on, Sidney. I'm not stupid."

She tried to avoid his eyes.

"You aren't a teenager. You met a man, had sex, and now you're pregnant. You aren't married, but that's your issue, not theirs. Why wouldn't you tell them? I'm sure they will want to meet him." Although he tried, he couldn't keep the jealousy completely out of his voice.

"He's married," she answered, looking out the window.

"You're kidding, right?"

"No, and his wife is beautiful. He'll probably stay with her forever."

"He should! Marriage is forever. I thought you understood that. Why would you do that, Sid? What were you thinking?" He hit the dashboard and shook his head, stunned and disappointed.

"I didn't know he was married at first."

"And did finding out even slow you down?"

"Look, you don't know everything, Jon. Life isn't as simple as you would like to believe. When people are lonely, they do dumb things."

"Yeah, get a cat or join some sort of club or something. They don't try to make a life with a married man!"

"You don't understand."

"I guess I don't. I think you're better than that. I thought you wanted to be a wife, not destroy a wife."

"That's a bit harsh, don't you think?" She let her annoyance show.

Jon took a breath, clearly upset. "Look, Sid, you said I was your friend. I believe a friend tells you the truth even when it hurts. You know it was wrong or you wouldn't have gone to such great lengths to hide it. I just don't know if you know that you deserve to be loved. You don't deserve to be second place in any man's heart, and I hate to see you settle for less than you deserve." His voice grew softer. He sounded sincere, like he meant every word.

They both grew silent, frozen in some memory of who they'd once been; both wondering how they'd ever gotten to this place.

Jon wanted to put his arms around Sidney and hold her, but at the same time he was so disappointed in her. He had never felt so clueless about her. From the moment he met her he had been able to read her, stay a step ahead. She'd been wild and reckless in a way he had adored when they were teenagers. She'd been fun and free and unafraid. She had been easy to fall in love with.

Sidney and Jon had met at church. Jon's family was strict, and his parents were good parents, the kind of parents who expected and received obedience. They loved God and taught their children to love Him. They were good—definitely good. They were also definitely hard to please.

Jon's mother knew that Sidney was not the best influence on her son. Sidney was in church because her parents made her come. Jon's mom knew that Jon and Sidney together would mean nothing but trouble.

But Jon had taken a chance on Sidney, the way kids do when they're in love. He saw her heart, and he knew what she could be—what she really wanted to be if she were honest with herself.

It was winter when he broke up with her. They'd been together from their teen years into adulthood. Even as he said the words that ended their relationship, he still loved her.

He had felt he must choose between her and everything he knew about God. He couldn't be with her anymore and not be with her. But she wasn't ready to get married. She had goals for her life, and she felt that marrying Jon would be the end of her dreams. But for Jon it was all or nothing.

She had looked so beautiful that night, nestled into her coat at the red light. She slid off her shoe and laid her toes in his lap, tempting him. He was tempted to take her somewhere and take her out of that coat, her clothes, her everything. He wanted her so badly. But he took her home and said good-bye, shocking them both.

That was the past that lingered in his mind as he looked at her slightly pregnant form in the dark. That was the past that confused him in the moment and made them both a little sad.

Chapter Nine

BRAD'S EYES FLICKED from side to side beneath their lids. He was almost awake, but not quite. Jennifer hoped he wouldn't feel her watching him, studying every feature.

Today would mark their baby's conception. In a few hours, Nicole's egg and Brad's sperm would meet together to form the earliest existence of Sullivan Joseph or Sally Josephine Frank. They chose those names in honor of Brad's parents. Joseph and Sally had passed away in August two years earlier. They had meant so much to Brad that Jennifer wouldn't have contested naming their child after one of them even if she hadn't liked the names.

Nicole had been taking medicine to increase egg production. She seemed nervous but pretty committed to the process. She had signed a contract and tolerated a little queasiness from the hormones; other than that she'd been fantastic.

Brad called her their knight in shining stilettos, even though the three of them knew she would never be caught dead in shoes as painful as stilettos. Nicky was all about comfort, and she was giving up being comfortable to do this for them. Maybe she wasn't selfish after all. At least not when it really mattered.

His eyes opened, and he smiled at Jennifer and combed her face with his hand.

"You ready for this?" he asked, still smiling.

"It's really going to happen, honey. I still can't believe it."

He kissed her before throwing back the covers. He wasn't one for lingering in bed after he woke. If he was awake, he had to be doing something.

The retrieval would be done in the clinic in an hour's time. They would have to come home after the procedure and let the doctor do the magic.

Jennifer had dreamed of this day for quite some time.

She'd obsessed really, and the obsession had led her to a beautiful idea. She had taken a small sheet of card stock with baby footprints in pink and blue from the scrapbook store. She'd cut it down and saved it for this day to blot her lipstick on. She laminated it and planned to give it to the doctor doing the fertilization. It would be a kiss for her baby, with him or her from the very first moment of life—today, sometime around noon.

Nicky was awake, reading in the living room. She'd already showered and dressed and paced the floor a bit.

"Good morning, Mommy." She smiled. "I already had breakfast, so you don't need to go gourmet this morning."

"Speak for yourself!" Jennifer laughed and joined Nicky on the sofa.

"What are you reading?" Brad asked.

"The research suggestion Professor Marks gave for the internship. It's stupid to read it now, I know. But these people are so interesting."

"What people?" Jennifer felt guilty that she knew nothing about the dream Nicky was giving up for them.

"It's a couple who lived in the area during slavery. The woman was a homeopathic doctor. She had a huge collection of remedies in her cellar that stayed in the family for years, along with the house itself. Her descendants found writing on the inside label of one of the near-empty bottles, and it looks like it's a map. They called Dr. Saunders, the professor of archeology, and he got Professor Marks and a professor from the medical program to check it out. They think she may have been a doctor for the Underground Railroad or involved in it in some way."

"Wow! That's really cool," Brad said.

"Yeah, it is. It's making me crazy that I wasn't chosen to intern. I've researched it like crazy, and I think the contents of the bottles are actually clues. I don't know. It's just a theory, and I guess no one wants it anyway." Then she smiled. "You guys go get ready for your big day!"

She tried to smile again, but didn't quite pull it off. Her life had taken a sharp turn in a short amount of time. She was still adapting emotionally.

Kristen loved it when the waiting room was full. It made her feel powerful to know they were all waiting for her to call their names and lead them behind the door to their rooms. She paused over her clipboard until the entire room was watching her in suspense. Then she sauntered to the room two steps ahead of the patient, pretending her nurse's shoes were Prada and her pink scrubs a custom creation from Dior. She would close the door behind her after she led them into the empty room to begin the line of questioning. That's when her heart reminded her head that she was just a nurse on a busy day caring for vulnerable, emotional, worry-filled women who needed her to be their nurse, minus Prada and Dior. They needed her to care about them, and sometimes she truly did.

Today was one of those days. She almost regretted making lunch plans with Alexis, who would be arriving soon to pick Kristen up. Kristen could see the fear in the eyes of some of the patients that made her want to ignore the clock.

Nicole Bell, the chart said. She was a surrogate, but she looked pale and unsure. She was shaking—almost shivering—trying to disguise her lack of control by tapping her foot.

Kristen handed her a robe and instructed her to slip it on and have a seat. Nicole took the garment and looked up at Kristen.

"Can I ask you something?" she asked nervously.

"Sure. You can ask me anything, but the doctors are your best bet."

"Well, I just... I've never done this before. I mean, I'm not a mom yet. I don't have my own kids or anything. I just wonder... will I still be myself when this is over, after the baby? Because you know how moms say it changed the way they felt and thought afterwards. Will I be different?"

Kristen sat down beside her. "Experiences change us. They always do, sometimes for the better and sometimes not. You aren't the same person today as you were ten years ago. You've learned things, and you're continuing to grow and expand your thinking."

"What will I learn from this, though? I have a life, and everything is stopping for this. I love my friends, and I want to do this for them, but I like what I've got going for myself and I don't want to…" She faltered.

"Lose yourself in this process?"

Nicky nodded and held her breath.

"It sounds like you're asking for a personal opinion, so here's mine. You're right on the brink of something big. You have to follow your heart, but I do think you'll learn something big if you proceed today. That kind of sacrifice doesn't come easily. Have you prayed about it?"

"You know, I pray sometimes, and I prayed about this some, but God doesn't talk to me, or else I don't understand Him if He does." Nicky looked at her hands. "I wonder what God would think about all this. Does He think we're trying to do His job for Him? It's so hard to know what's right. I wish my friend could have her own baby, and life could be easy."

"Sure you do. It's right to want that, but life gets challenging. Sometimes we have no choice, even when we have one, because the love is too strong to ignore. God knows you inside, Nicole. You're laying down your life—the next few months anyway—for your friend. I think God smiles at that selflessness."

Kristen went to the sink, filled a paper cup with water, and handed it to her patient.

"You'll be okay. Take a minute, drink some water, and change your clothes. The doctor will be in soon. Whatever you do today, you're different, okay?"

Kristen smiled as she left the room and winked at the anxious parents-to-be in the waiting room.

Alexis wasn't crying when she woke up this morning. She was, for once, thinking clearly and remembering her life back home that she had simply up and left. People must be wondering about her. Maybe they were calling to check up on her, especially the ones who really knew her.

She called home and entered the code for her messages to be played, optimistic and eager to hear the voice of a familiar friend.

The first message was from Peter. "Can you just listen to me, Alexis? There's stuff you don't know or understand and things you've thought you know that you don't. Walking away isn't going to fix this. It's our life, and I don't want to live it without you."

She couldn't believe what he was saying. He'd had her there all along and it had never been enough. She felt as if she had been living alone, fighting for their marriage all by herself, while he was playing house with another woman. It made her laugh—a bitter, angry laugh.

Then the next message started. Alexis stiffened at the sound of the voice before the recognition even registered.

"So I know you guys must be fixing stuff. Whatever, it's fine. I know I might end up alone, and it's a chance I took, but I'm not calling to try and see you, Peter. I'm calling about the baby. There's something's wrong with the baby. I wanted to tell you in person and not talk to a machine. I don't want to lose my baby, Peter. It doesn't have to be yours. It's mine. I get that. But, God, can't you return a phone call!" The message cut off and started fresh a moment later.

"It's something to do with his heart, I think. The doctor was very vague and is sending me to a specialist. I need to know about Zeek. I need you to tell me. I'm at my parents' house, but they don't know about you, so my cell is the only way to reach me. I'm scheduled to see a Dr. Fletcher here. I hear she's good and maybe she can help, but Peter... I... I'm sorry. If you guys are fixing things, you don't have to call me. Just call the doctor, or fax her the information. Please!"

The message cut out again then returned with Sidney, barely hanging on. "Peter, please. I'm begging. Call the doctor, area code 515-555-8222. Get the fax number if you'd rather. My appointment is the twelfth at eleven o'clock at Corbin Bridge Health Clinic in the east wing, office 216 for fertility and high-risk pregnancy. They think I'm high risk. Please call, Peter."

Then a dial tone.

At first, Alexis was frozen by it, cold and emotionless, until she heard her son's name and felt the panic in the other woman's voice.

She was paralyzed by confusion. In that moment there was no other woman. They were both women. They were two hurting women, needing the same reassurance, forgiveness, and support from the same man. If Peter wouldn't go, she should. That's the way she felt, even though she didn't know why. How could such a thought even occur to her? Then she heard the name of the office and the butterflies of irony made her run to the bathroom to vomit and tremble and cry.

Sidney was here, in this city, at that office, and her sister could be looking at that child on a monitor at this moment. Today was the twelfth.

Where is Peter? She tried his cell phone over and over, then his work, and finally Eric's house. That's where he had been only a day ago. Was he coming? Did he know? Was he okay?

She felt sick inside for the husband she hadn't wanted to love. She knew the hurt he would feel and wanted to be with him. She wanted to know he was okay. Beyond that, she didn't know what she felt. She just wanted him to be okay, both physically and emotionally.

She was throwing on clothes when the doorbell rang. She answered it to find Peter standing before her.

"I'm not waiting for you anymore," he said. "You won't come back, so I came to you. I need you Alexis. I was a stupid fool, and I've made a mess of everything, I know. I wish I could change everything, but time doesn't work that way."

"Come inside," she said.

"Alexis, I treated you horribly. I was unfaithful. I—"

"Listen to me, Peter. Have you spoken to Sidney?"

"I'm trying to tell you. She was the only one I slept with. I haven't seen her or spoken to her since before you left. It's over. I can't hurt you or myself like this anymore."

"You don't know."

"Know what?"

"She's been trying to reach you. There are complications with the baby. Possibly his heart."

"Oh, God!" Peter cried and held her. "It was me. It was *my* fault that Zeek was sick."

He backed away from her, dropping into a chair and crying into his hands.

Compassion overrode her disappointment, and she squatted down to see his face, finally understanding the guilt he felt about Zeek. She took a minute, a private minute with her husband, then led him to the car and drove him to the clinic. She took the time to tell him there had been no blame, only loneliness.

She had no interest in why Zeek was gone. It would make her crazy. She only wanted someone to hold her when she hurt and love her when she couldn't love back. She needed someone strong enough to feel with her and not run from the pain. She didn't want to share him, and she didn't want to lose him, but she wouldn't lose herself either. She had to have something; loyalty would be a start.

She walked through the door first, and Kristen tried to disguise the shock when she saw him. Then she eyed him skeptically when she saw her sister's pink face following him.

"Everything okay?" she asked.

"We need to know if Sidney Flannery is still here," Alexis said.

"Yes." Kristen looked at them quizzically.

"I'm her baby's father. Let me go to her," Peter said.

Jon waited in the lobby, reading an outdated *Newsweek*. He had wanted to go back with Sidney, but she'd insisted he wait, and he graciously accepted her wishes.

Jon was content to be Sidney's moral support if she decided she needed him. She looked so nervous lately. She spent most of her days sprawled on the couch at Jon's apartment. It was a refuge when she didn't have the courage to come clean to her family. She slept at home and stayed away the rest of the time, avoiding conversation with her parents.

This morning Jon had picked her up early. Mr. Flannery was sitting at the table, drinking coffee and reading the paper. He answered the door after Jon's first knock.

Sidney was in the bathroom, so Mr. Flannery took advantage of the opportunity to question Jon. "Is she okay?" he asked.

Jon looked at him, deciding how to answer.

"I can't tell what's wrong," Mr. Flannery said. "She says she's feeling fine, but she gets upset when I ask questions. I'm worried about her. It's not like her to pull away from me, you know?"

Jon nodded and looked down the hallway to make sure Sidney wasn't coming. He could see that her dad was legitimately worried, and Jon couldn't ignore him.

"Your daughter is taking me back as a friend, and I can't risk destroying that. She needs a friend right now. I'm looking out for her, and I can promise you she will come to you when she is ready."

Mr. Flannery raised his eyebrow in concern.

"She'll be okay. Don't worry." He could hear Sidney coming.

Jon and Sidney ate breakfast at Jon's apartment. He served her blueberry muffins, orange juice, and a banana. He insisted that she eat everything.

His apartment was masculine but inviting. Christian music played in the background. It soothed her and shamed her at the same time. It was strange how she remembered some songs—songs she hadn't heard in years:

You're all I want. You're all I've ever needed. You're all I want, help me know you are near. The chorus played again and again, until finally she grew the courage to question it.

"Do you think it's really enough?" she asked, "Just God? Just knowing He's near? I need something I can touch, someone to touch me back. Someone to reassure me. I need an actual voice."

"That's what's wrong, Sid," Jon answered, "You need to listen."

"Listen to what?"

"You need to stop looking for a man to rescue you."

"Excuse me?"

"I mean, you'd choose Jesus the man over Jesus the man who is fully God. You'd settle for a physical man when Jesus wants to meet your physical and spiritual needs."

"He seems so far away," she said quietly.

"He is always with you, Sid. He'll be with you today too. You can't disappoint Him enough to make Him stop loving you."

Jon held Sidney's soft hands in his and prayed with her before they left for the clinic. He'd seen something in her eyes that seemed bright, even hopeful. Life was returning to her eyes.

He held her hand again in the car when they arrived. She was afraid and absorbed in her unborn child, and he loved her again—if he'd ever really stopped. There was stillness between them that could have been filled with a kiss but instead was sealed with an encouraging smile from him.

Now he waited alone patiently, pretending to read old news. Then he heard someone ask about Sidney, someone claiming to be the baby's father. Jon wasn't ordinarily confrontational. In fact, he was so laid back that sometimes he could seem uncaring. But not today. Not after listening to Sidney cry and plead into the phone for two days for this man to simply answer a question.

Sidney had disappointed Jon for sure, abandoning her morals for this man. Somehow Jon tended to believe the man was more at fault in these situations. The guy should never have betrayed his wife, no matter how flirtatious Sidney had been. He should have stopped it and walked away. Instead, he'd encouraged her, used her, and abandoned her. Jon had no respect for him.

He slammed his magazine down on the table and walked over to the man. "Did you say you were looking for Sidney?" he asked accusingly.

Peter looked at him, clearly wondering who he was and why he cared. "Yes." He sounded unsure of himself.

"You're Peter?" Jon snapped.

Peter nodded slightly and looked at Kristen with a puzzled expression. He had barely turned his head when Jon threw him against the wall.

"Where the hell have you been?" Jon's eyes were hot.

Another man, who was waiting for his wife, jumped up and held Jon back, pulling him from the room and giving Kristen time to quickly usher Peter and Alexis into the main office.

Kristen took Alexis into a private room and led Peter to the room where Sidney sat waiting on the exam table. Her eyes were red and swollen from her tears.

Peter introduced himself to the doctor, shaking hands as he apologized to Sidney. "I just heard your message. I had no idea this was happening, or I would have been here sooner."

Dr. Fletcher motioned him to take a seat. "It's good that you came. Any history you can give us would be helpful."

"My son, Zeek, died when he was three from heart complications. He was born with holes in his heart that required surgery. He... uh... he had two surgeries. The first one seemed to work for a while, then they found a blockage and had to go back in and repair an artery. That might have worked, but he reacted to the anesthesia. It caused heart palpitations, and his heart was too weak to handle it. It was too much stress on his heart."

"Did anyone else have heart trouble in your family" the doctor asked.

"I have a mild arrhythmia, nothing major. But my father has had a heart attack."

"We believe that we have located the problem. When Sidney first came in, a few days ago, she was experiencing some cramping and the nurse performed an ultrasound. Looking at the ultrasound I agreed with the findings that the baby has a single umbilical artery. This can mean a wide range of possibilities. There is an increased risk of stillbirth and I'll want to perform some tests to rule out possible abnormalities. An amniocentesis is a good start. I'll be looking for any abnormalities with the heart, brain, gastrointestinal tract, urinary tract, or in the bones. I'll be watching her closely."

The doctor turned to her patient. "Sidney, you must try to stay calm. If your blood pressure goes up, that could exacerbate the problem, so I need you to try your best to relax. I don't want you to fly. Stay with your family or whatever you need to do, but stay off your feet and stay local. We'll have to wait and see. Increase liquids. I don't want you to slack at all on water, okay? Eat several small meals throughout the day and keep weekly appointments. The odds of survival are improving and with close monitoring we should be able to prevent some risk to the baby. I actually believe that your stomach pain was unrelated, maybe indigestion or a slight touch of the flu. In any case it was a blessing that you came in. Because of that we were able to detect this problem early. Normal delivery should be possible, but early delivery and low birthweight are some things you should be prepared for. Any questions?"

"Are you worried about a miscarriage?" Peter asked.

"Sidney and I have discussed that possibility. She's aware of what to watch for, and we are going to do our best for her and the baby."

Sidney stared straight ahead. She wanted her clothes on. She wanted a bed in a room behind a closed door where she could cry herself to sleep and not worry about witnesses.

"In the event that a caesarean is needed, I will talk to an anesthesiologist prior. We'll want to make sure we don't use whatever anesthetic your son had a reaction to. It's unlikely that she'll need a caesarean or that the baby would have your son's reaction, but we will take every precaution." Dr. Fletcher stood up and handed Sidney her checkout slip.

"It's good to meet you," she said to Peter. "She's going to need a lot of support."

She told Sidney to make another appointment in a week and directed Peter to come along if he was able.

Sidney began dressing, feeling uncomfortable with Peter there. She could tell that Peter felt awkward, as well.

"I really am sorry. I wasn't ignoring your calls, I promise," he said quietly.

"She knows about me," Sidney said as she pulled on her shoes.

"She's outside," he answered.

"It's over then?" She kept her eyes on her shoes, not wanting to see what his eyes might be saying.

"Yeah," he said softly. "In some ways it's over. Sidney, I'm just a stupid guy who has hurt a lot of people trying to run from my own pain. I've got to make it work with Alexis. I've got to be fair."

"What, then? Do you want to be in the baby's life at all? Would Alexis? I don't know where we go from here."

"I don't want to sound uncaring; I want the baby to make it, and I hope you know that."

"What do you want me to do?" She was frustrated and tired.

"I want you to go home with the man in the waiting room, who I think wants my head on a silver platter. Call me when our child is born or if there's a problem. I want you to understand that I didn't mean for any of this to happen."

"And it might not," she said bitterly.

"Don't. Don't imply that I would wish this. I'm a jerk, Sidney, but I'm not that cold."

"Fine. I'll call you when the baby is born, or *if* the baby is born. Good-bye." She headed to the door.

Peter grabbed her hand gently one last time and whispered, "I'm sorry" into her hair before Sidney left the room and the office on the arm of another man.

Chapter Ten

THEY SAT PATIENTLY in the lobby, passing the time playing footsy and being silent together. Brad had been cool and steady through everything. It had been a surprise—even to him—the way his nerves had unraveled as he parked the car. He was afraid but determined to play the role of optimist, encourager, and friend.

He was afraid that disappointment was around the corner or that a black mark would slash across a lifelong friendship. He wanted it to work, but he was afraid of that too. What if he became second place in Jennifer's heart? What would a baby mean for their relationship? He was afraid of the change and the responsibility. Yet he wanted this. Even as his hands shook, he imagined tiny fingers wrapped around his.

Everyone knew he would be a fantastic dad. His employees at the restaurant had joked that God made Jennifer infertile out of love for every other father out there who would never be able to be as fantastic at fathering as Brad would be. He'd taken it good naturedly, wondering what role God really took in infertility.

A baby was the only thing Jennifer wanted that he couldn't give her. Quietly, selfishly, Brad had enjoyed having her all to himself.

She was nervous too—excited but nervous. She winked at him each time their eyes met, and she bit her nails as if they were dipped in chocolate.

"Will you quit?" he said when he couldn't take the click of the biting anymore. "What will be left to run down my back when we celebrate?" he whispered.

"I'm so nervous. I can't help it," she answered.

She was holding Nicky's cell phone in her purse, and she pulled it out and looked at Brad.

"Do you think she'd mind if I play a game on it?"

"No. She doesn't have any secrets from you, and you're just playing games, right?"

Jennifer walked over to the far side of the lobby where cell phones wouldn't affect the medical equipment and began a quick game of Tetris.

The cell phone buzzed, startling her.

"Hello? Nicky Bell's phone." She shrugged her shoulders at Brad who was shaking his head at her from across the room.

"Nicky?"

"No. This is her friend. Can I take a message?" she offered politely.

"Yes. This is Becky Cunningham. I'm calling on behalf of Professor Marks to inform her that she's been accepted as an intern."

Jennifer stood up, the phone pressed to her ear. "Wait! That doesn't make sense. She's already been turned down. Someone else—a sophomore or something was chosen instead."

"Yes. Well, actually, Professor Marks referred her to the anthropology department, and they all agreed that she was more qualified than any of the other applicants. This internship won't be directly under Professor Marks. It's more like a field study in anthropology, but if she wants it, it's hers. If she has any questions just tell her to call Becky."

"Yes. Okay. I'll let her know."

Jennifer walked directly to the waiting room window and asked for a nurse.

"What's wrong?" Brad was at her side.

"I've got to see Nicky. We have to stop this," she said as the secretary buzzed her through the door.

A nurse led her back and tapped on the door before letting her enter. The room was empty, and Nicky was sitting on the exam table in the gown, expecting to see the doctor.

"It's okay, Nicky," Jennifer said. "Let's just go. You don't have to do this."

"What?" Nicky looked bewildered.

"Someone named Becky just called for you. They've given you the internship. It's what you've worked for. I can't ask you to do this now." Jennifer tried to control her disappointment, stiffening every muscle and ignoring the sting in her eyes as she blinked tears away.

"Come here," Nicky said. She reached out and pulled Jennifer close. Jennifer's tears rolled onto the shoulder of Nicky's gown.

"This is more important," Nicky said. "*You* are more important. I have a ton of doors open to me after this, but you have one. Jennifer, you need to be a mommy. That's all you've ever wanted."

"It can wait. I can wait."

"I can't. I'm not getting any younger. I'm here now. I'm ready to do this for you. I've got eggs in me that desperately want to make you a mommy. They have been multiplying like gangbusters especially for this day. I've given up my apartment."

"What?"

"Well, I can't commute, silly!" She laughed. "I'm here now. This is my life now. The rest can wait."

"Seriously?" Jennifer was amazed.

"Seriously. Now get out of here! I'm already psyched enough. I don't need to worry about what you think of me in this hideous thing." She smiled and pulled at the paisley hospital gown. "Okay? Now go!"

Jennifer hugged her tightly, and they both sighed with relief. Jennifer returned to the mauve waiting room and Brad's panicked expression.

After half an hour in the hallway talking to a guy from their church and the perplexing moments when he wondered if the whole plan was falling apart, Brad was exhausted.

He drove Jennifer and Nicky home, all three of them longing for naps. They were all so worn out they almost forgot about the laminated kiss in Dr. Olsander's pocket.

Chapter Eleven

"WHAT IS GOING on?" Kristen demanded as the door shut behind her.

"You won't believe it."

"Try me." Kristen sat down next to her sister.

"I guess Peter's other woman lives here now. Her family is from here. Can you believe it? I try to escape this mess, and it followed me here!"

"Maybe you're not supposed to escape it."

Alexis rolled her eyes, hating the idea that any good could come of this.

"Really, listen," Kristen continued. "Maybe God has a reason for making you face this."

"Don't make this a God thing, okay? Don't give me another reason to be mad at Him."

Kristen handed her sister a tissue and waited patiently.

"What's happening with Peter? Is he here for you or her?"

"He came for me, and I took him to *her*. Am I stupid or what?"

Kristen didn't answer. She just sat quietly and listened. Listening was something she was good at.

"She left this message, and... I don't know. She just sounded so afraid. I remember that fear from when I was pregnant with Zeek. I actually wanted to help her. It's insane, Kris. This woman is tearing my husband away from me. She's taking away the only thing I have left. I should hate her. I should want her to disappear, let her baby die or whatever. I don't know. I just can't think like that. I can't wish it on anyone, even *her*. She doesn't deserve my sympathy though. I hate that I feel it."

"Are you going to talk to him?" Kristen asked.

"Yeah. I mean, I guess so. He said that he's sorry. He wants to try to fix our relationship. It's just that everything is different now. She's having his child. He's part of a family that I can never be in. His being sorry won't fix that."

"Does he want to be with her?"

"It doesn't matter anymore, does it? She's the mother of his child. She'll always be there."

"What are you going to do?"

"Rain-check lunch and take him back to your place to talk. Is that okay?"

"Of course. I'll pray for you."

"Your prayers don't work, so don't bother," Alexis snapped.

"Excuse me? My prayers don't work?" Kristen's eyebrows shot clear into her hairline. She hated that Alexis rejected God after she had experienced Him so long. She knew that Zeek's death had robbed every drop of faith from Alexis' heart, but Alexis had no right to cast doubts on her sister's faith or the effectiveness of her prayers. It wouldn't be tolerated. For good or bad, Kristen knew God was listening to her. She wasn't about to let anyone cause her to doubt it.

It was true that some of her prayers hadn't been answered the way she would have liked. For instance, her prayers for Zeek. She had prayed for healing for her boy. Her whole church had prayed for him, and Kristen really believed he would be okay. His death pulled the rug out from under her. She had battled God over it, wrestling with Him in her heart until it was resolved. Zeek wasn't coming back. That was a fact nothing could change, but her attitude had. Zeek was with God now. What better healing could there be than that? Things had not gone the way she wanted, but if it was what God wanted, she would accept it. She wanted God's will to be done above everything.

Kristen had not asked God to do anything her way since. She talked to Him and confided her fears and troubles, she laid them at His feet, trusting that He knew what was best and would cause it to happen. She trusted that He would make everything right.

"You can let your marriage self-destruct if it's what you want, Alexis. You can spit in God's face every single day. You can hate Him and mock him. Mock me. Just know that without Him your marriage doesn't have a shot, and you know it. I will pray, because God hears my prayers. Things might seem to get worse, and it might take time, but you will love God again. I believe it, and I know that it's His will that all love Him. And that includes you. Challenge me if you want, but be smart enough not to challenge God." Kristen felt firm, confident, and decided. "I'll grab take-out and see you at dinner, okay? Don't take the next plane home or anything—let Peter earn you back."

"Okay." Alexis held the tissue to her nose. "I'm sorry."

Kristen hugged her and escorted her back to Peter.

He wasn't brave enough to meet her eyes.

Alexis made Peter take his shoes off at the door and got herself a glass of water at the sink before joining him on the couch.

"You came to me, so if you have something to say, go ahead." Her tone was sarcastic.

"You didn't tell me you were leaving," he said.

"Well, you didn't tell me you were having a child without me!"

"You have every right to be angry. I need help, Alexis. I'm falling apart, and I've been too stubborn to admit it."

"I won't let you blame Zeek for what you've done."

"No, that's not what I'm saying. You shouldn't let me blame him. It wasn't his fault. He didn't betray you—he didn't choose to die. But he is part of what I'm feeling. I haven't been myself since he died. I haven't coped with it rationally. You and I didn't go through it together the way we should have. We walled ourselves off, and… I don't know. I couldn't look at you. I couldn't see you and not think of him."

"That isn't my fault," Alexis interrupted him, "I didn't want him to die either."

He put his hand on hers and for a moment she let it rest there before pulling away.

"I know you didn't want that," he said. "That's not what I mean at all. He was our child, a dream we built together. I felt as if I wrecked it all. His heart problem came from me, from my family. I was so sure you blamed me. I couldn't face you. I was sure you would begin to hate me, and I punished you." Peter's eyes were red; she knew he was about to cry.

"I didn't blame you!" Alexis cried. "I just wanted you to share the pain with me, let me in. I lost both of you."

"I am so sorry. With Sidney... I was so arrogant. She didn't even know I was married at first. I wanted to forget that I had a life already, and I wanted to forget you because it hurt so much. So I lied. I lied a lot."

"Why didn't you come to me? Why did you make me look like such a fool?"

"You were distant. I thought maybe you didn't care anymore. You were always gone," he answered.

"I was avoiding the silence, Peter. You didn't talk to me."

"I know. I need you to know where I was when you left. I wasn't with her, or anyone, romantically. I found out about the baby and at first I was"—he looked at her briefly, feeling ashamed—"I was happy at first. Then she implied that it was a boy, and I... I don't know. I started pushing her away too. I was so angry. I went to the hospital. I knew it was stupid, but I wanted to be close to Zeek. I walked to his room. Remember the room? It was etched in my brain. I had to be there. I had to look at it again to see if any piece of him was still in that room somehow." He was choking up, and she was very silent.

"I knocked on the door and there was a boy—a little boy—lying in the bed. Only he wasn't Zeek. He was lonely. His parents had gone for food. He thought I was a volunteer, and I couldn't tell him the truth. I got the dry erase pen, and I drew a picture for him on his board, the way I did for Zeek. He smiled so big, and I began to remember everything. Our dreams, who I was, who you are. Everything. I was shopping for charcoal, not sleeping with another woman. I volunteered at the hospital. I've been drawing portraits for the kids, for their parents, really. Those kids are dying, and they made me understand that I am dying too."

"I know I pulled away," Alexis said. "I even considered an affair myself."

Pain crossed his face, and he hung his head.

"We need counseling if we're going to save our marriage."

"I know," he answered.

"What about *her?*"

"It's over."

"It can't be over. She's having a baby."

"I told her to call me when it's born. I figure by then we'll know about us. I'll do whatever you want. I'll have to pay child support; I owe them that. I won't see the baby, though, if you ask me not to. I'll bring you to see it if you want. It's your decision. I want our marriage to work. I'm putting you first. I just hope it's not too late."

Alexis began to cry, and she let him hold her. The flood of hurt they'd kept from each other was unleashed, and they sat that way for a long time.

Chapter Twelve

IT WAS LUNCH time and Kristen's stomach was growling, begging to be fed something rich and wonderful. She didn't have time for wonderful today. There was no point, now that she would be eating alone. She was sick of eating alone, sick of being alone and waiting to be noticed, sick of waiting to be loved by someone eager to share each day with her. She wondered why things never seemed to work out for her. When she was a girl, the boys had loved her. They thought of her as just one of the guys. They knew she could whip them at nearly every sport, and they respected her for it. They included her in their games, and they never seemed to notice that she was a girl.

But the other girls noticed. Kristen was too beautiful for the girls to ignore.

The boys didn't notice her shiny, long hair hidden under her dad's old cap. They didn't notice the sparkle in her eyes and her flawless complexion. They were distracted by their own male pride and competitive drive. That is until Kristen began to get a figure.

Suddenly she was no longer one of the boys, and none of the girls she knew—except for her sister—could put aside their jealousy to be friends with her.

Maybe that's why she had chosen this particular field of medicine. Maybe it made her feel powerful to see other women feeling uncomfortable, nervous, and insecure. She knew they were silently comparing themselves to her, even as she was wishing to be them.

Why couldn't she be content? She was so restless, taking on other people's problems, worming her way into other people's lives. She cared even when she didn't want to care. In a way she had begun to crave the chaos in other people's lives. She was happy for the mess, a reason to be needed, and a reason to exist.

She decided she would indulge herself with a brownie from the bakery or maybe something from the chocolate shop located in the mall. She was thinking about which delight she could devour the quickest as she unlocked her car door.

"Hey! You leaving?" She heard a male voice yell from a few spots away. "Kristen! Are you leaving already?"

She turned to find Joey Bentley grinning at her.

"What are you doing here?" she asked.

"I like to hang out at the gyno from time to time, maybe pick up some chicks." He laughed at her look of disbelief. "What? You don't think it's possible?"

She shook her head.

"Yeah, I guess it is a little bit of a stretch. The truth is that I'm the hazard man for Corbin Bridge."

"Well, they're bubbling over in there with hazardous material. You'll have your work cut out."

"Actually, I just picked up for this route. I'm all alone playing garbage boy today. You want to get a bite to eat, catch up? Or are you still on the clock?"

"I'm off the clock for about forty-five minutes." She decided to forget about the chocolate. They agreed to drive separately.

He parked his car next to hers when they arrived at the restaurant at the same time. He was out of his car and opening her door before she got her keys out of the ignition.

"So, when did you move back?" Kristen asked, stabbing her fork into the lettuce on her plate.

"I've been around. Well, let's see. First, I was in California—"

"Oh, yeah. I remember you wanted to get into acting. I got some very entertaining letters back then." She laughed.

"Right. Well, when I finally recognized what a failure I was at that, I left California and followed a girlfriend out to Washington. Her dad owned a fish shop in Seattle, and I went to work for him."

"Really! Did you have to chuck headless fish at tourists and stuff?"

"No. I was the one who beheaded them. Not a glamorous job. My ego was totally fried. The girlfriend dropped me for some longhaired Kurt Cobain wannabe, and I was pretty destroyed."

"Well, what a fun lunch this is turning out to be!" Kristen teased.

"You ought to try living it! Anyway I finally cashed in my pride and came back home. I stayed with my brother, got a respectable degree, and wound up collecting used needles from local doctors' offices." He laughed as he raised his arms in mock surrender.

"I guess by the time we get to our age we've pretty much figured out what reality can do to our dreams."

"It's not all bad though," he said. "This job, as boring as it is, pays the bills. I've got evenings and weekends off to 'trod the boards.' I've done a few voiceovers. I still get to do a few of the things I like. How about you? I know you're a nurse, but you still play ball on the weekends and stuff, right?"

Kristen laughed at the idea, picturing herself attempting to make a basket and breaking a hip.

"Uh… no. I don't do sports anymore."

"Not at all?" Joey looked surprised and a little sad.

"I'm a grown-up now. I don't have time for games. Who I was then isn't necessarily who I am now."

Joey looked at Kristen's white clogs tapping the floor. He remembered the black Adidas. Her hair was silky and shorter now, just skimming her shoulders and curled up on the ends. Womanly. In his mind he could still see her stringy black hair pulled up in a ponytail and flapping behind her as she maneuvered through the court to make a play.

He'd been to every game his old clunker could get him to—watching her and cheering her on, and falling in love with who she was then. Apparently she was no longer that person.

It was strange how he had zeroed in on her in those days. She was the jock in a family devoted to the arts; the red ball in a bag of jacks. She stood out.

It was weird how they met. He was planning to be an actor. His high school years were spent poring over scripts for local community theater auditions. He had met Kristen's sister first, naturally. Alexis had been a school favorite when it came to the arts. In fact, she was voted "most artistic" by her senior class.

He and Alexis had been paired up frequently as romantic counterparts, and if he was honest he'd have to admit he'd kissed her more times than any other girl during those four years. But there had been only friendship between them. Just business, despite what the audience believed.

His first encounter with Kristen would have stopped most guys in their tracks. She was full of fire and as protective of Alexis as a mama grizzly. She had come around to the back of the theater during intermission. It was early spring, and the actors enjoyed playing cards and drinking coca-cola in the parking lot between stage appearances.

He and Alexis were sitting on top of his car with their legs dangling over the windshield, smoking cigarettes and soaking up the sun. When Kristen saw them, her eyes were brighter than the sun, certainly hotter. The roof popped as they jumped off.

"This is my sister, Kristen," Alexis introduced. "Kristen, this is Joey Bentley."

"Joey Bentley, don't you know that you're too young to corrupt yourself and my sister with cancer sticks?"

She was so uptight it was almost funny, though he didn't dare laugh. She was the good girl, the straight-laced, straight-A student; the perfect child who was dying to be seen, desperate for approval, and too different to be understood. But from that day on, Joey Bentley was on a mission to understand the prima donna with the blazing eyes.

At first it was an experiment to see if he could make a nice girl turn not-so-nice. But he lost interest in that quickly.

He searched for her face in the audience as he delivered heartfelt monologues onstage, and he lingered next to Alexis after the curtain calls, hoping Kristen would come backstage. He attended her games, hoping to find the place where she relaxed. But if there was such a place, that wasn't it. She was competitive. It wasn't about having fun to her; it was about winning. It was about cheers and victory. So he cheered loudly.

Kristen intimidated him. It was silly how he'd let himself obsess over her. She could have any guy she wanted, and she knew all their trade secrets. She was like one of the guys.

There had been one summer just before his senior year when Alexis threw a party at her house. Some of the guys started playing basketball, and or course Kristen was allowed into the game. He had played, too, at her request, hoping not to humiliate himself with his lack of knowledge of the sport. He wanted to impress her, so he played hard. He competed against her aggressively, too aggressively maybe. He had embarrassed her, accidentally brushing his hand against her chest. They had both blushed.

The following year she avoided him. She was struggling to belong that year. Searching for who she was while everyone else was determining who they were going to be. He still noticed her and was still distracted by her, hoping for the opportunity to steal her first kiss.

After lunch, Joey gave Kristen his number. She smirked to herself as she watched his truck turn out of the lot, orange hazard bags filling up the passenger seat. He'd always been a hazard. She couldn't decide if he was a temptation or a trap. He'd been risky and flirty and dangerous before. He still seemed different, and she laughed to herself about the change. Joey Bentley had prayed a truce over their meal! An unforced, not-out-of-habit, sincere, heartfelt prayer. He was so different now!

Maybe she would call him.

Chapter Thirteen

JON DROVE QUIETLY back to his apartment while Sidney sobbed into a disintegrating, pink tissue.

"You're not taking me back to my parents?" she asked when she looked up and saw they were pulling up to his place. "I thought you'd take me home and tell them my secret and walk out on me for good."

"I thought you'd hate me for threatening Peter! I wanted to beat up the guy you've been crying about."

"I'm not crying about Peter!" she defended quickly. "I don't need Peter."

"Then why the tears?"

"Jon, I'm pregnant, and my baby doesn't have a daddy. Peter will do what he has to, but not out of love. Just because he feels obligated. And *I* did this! I feel stupid, okay? Stupid and embarrassed. His wife brought him there. Why would she do that? I wouldn't have done that. I feel guilty, okay? I had convinced myself, even after I heard her on the phone, that I wasn't to blame; that no one was hurt who didn't deserve it anyway. I was so wrong. Everyone is hurt, and it's my fault!"

She began to cry again. "I'm not crying because I was rejected. If he had rejected me sooner I wouldn't be in this position. I just hate being somebody's mistake."

"You made a mistake; that doesn't make *you* a mistake," Jon said. "Let's talk inside. The neighbors will think we're nuts."

They went inside and he handed her a square box of blue tissues he kept on hand for the singles' Bible study he led. Emotions often ran high during those weekly studies, and he had learned to be prepared.

"Why did you want to hurt Peter and not me?" Sidney asked. "I mean, I asked for it, didn't I?"

"Sidney, don't ask me that, okay? I know it was stupid. Let's just leave it at that."

"Stupid and kind of sweet. I never expected you to stand up for me like that." She climbed up on the kitchen stool and watched as he put water in the kettle and turned the stove on.

"Why not?"

"Because we have such a confusing history. In love, out of love. Working, not working. Friends, and almost strangers. I was never what you wanted me to be, and I didn't think you'd defend me."

"Stop thinking you have me figured out, Sidney. You don't know what I'm feeling."

"Well, tell me then. What are you feeling?"

"For one thing, you were everything I wanted you to be. I was crazy in love with you. I wanted to marry you, but… never mind. Just forget I said anything. Do you want tea or hot chocolate?"

"Say what you were going to say. Why did you decide you didn't want to marry me?" Sidney's eyes burrowed into John's soul and tore at his heart.

He poured the steaming water down the drain and set the pot in the sink. Then he leaned over the counter, covering his face with his hands. "You weren't serious," he said softly. "You wanted to play, and I didn't want to pretend with you. God mattered to me, and you were wrestling against Him. We weren't enough for you. You'd have said no anyway."

"How do you know what I'd have said?"

"I know."

"And now I'm not good enough to date! I'm damaged goods, still wrestling with God, and pregnant."

"So you screwed up," Jon said. "Get over it. This baby is about the only thing you've done right in all of this. You could have chosen an abortion, but you didn't. You felt love for this baby even if it meant losing your own sources of love. I'm proud of you for choosing to be a mom. I didn't stop loving you when you walked out of my life, and I didn't stop when you came back into it."

"But everything's different. I'm not good enough for you. I'm never going to be."

Before she could go any further, Jon jumped the counter. He put his hand under her chin, tipped her head back, and kissed her. He held her face in his hands. "I wanted to hurt Peter because I'm jealous that he loved you like I never could."

"He didn't. No one has loved me like you."

He let her go and she followed him into the living room.

"Are you sorry you did that?" she asked.

"No. Are you sorry that it's going to end there?"

"Why does it have to?"

"Because you have to sort yourself out with God before I can really matter to you—before I *should* matter to you. You don't need anyone to forgive you but Him. Don't you realize that? I didn't give up on you. I still love you. God still loves you too. But you're still ignoring Him, and I'm still waiting. Eventually you're going to run out of time."

Mr. Flannery was napping behind his newspaper when Sidney got home from Jon's. He looked up when he heard her.

"Where's Mom?" she asked.

"Last I knew she was headed to lunch with some ladies and then up to the church to quilt."

"Go back to your nap, Dad. I think I'd like a little nap myself." She headed up to her childhood room. The walls were taupe now, but she could swear she saw little flecks of Pepto-Bismol pink peeking through from when it had been her room. The room had changed with her. If she thought about it, the room had maybe matured a little faster.

She had fought adulthood with everything inside her. Even her important corporate job hadn't tamed her. Early in her life she had promised herself to never wear gray or sit in front of a computer in a cubicle and resign herself to a boring, straight-laced, grown-up life. She wanted to always be fun and spontaneous. She would wear hot pink shoes on rainy days and decorate her wall with a pink boa and empty gum packets tied together with string to make a garland. It was a reminder to relax, to not get lost in her job. She had been acting like a child pretending to be an adult.

The room had been transformed the week after she moved out. The room was no longer a little girl. It was now a woman, wise and sophisticated, understated and grandmotherly. The room had outgrown her, but it still remembered. There was a box on the bed. A present wrapped in pastel-colored baby footprints. She tore at the paper and opened the box, loving her mom as the suspense built. How had she known Sidney would need a surprise today? Something sweet and wonderful to remind her of the life growing inside her, beautiful and alive.

Inside the wrapping paper was a pink plastic Barbie case with a silver latch on the side. She opened it and a parade of pink fluff and tiny sparkle shoes covered the bed. The Barbie dolls inside had been hers. Barbie was something Sidney had tried to be but couldn't—an adult but also a child. She was something Sidney had tried to be and failed. Barbie was an adult, but also a child. She was a valuable collectable to adults but left outside in the sandbox by kids. She appealed to everyone. She was innocent and naïve while being womanly and sexual. She was everyone and no one. She was Barbie, plastic and impossible.

There were a couple of blue Hotwheels that had belonged to Mitchell. The wheels bent outward from the weight and force of his hand racing them on the kitchen floor.

There was also a small, transparent bag with pink-and-blue rope and a wood block with holes forming a heart. It was a lace-up. She remembered sitting on the floor and working the rope through the holes as she pretended to sew as her mother tapped the pedal on her sewing machine. She found a collection of comics that Dad had clipped from every newspaper since she'd announced her pregnancy. Finally, she saw the card, and she smiled at her family's love.

> *Honey, these are just little trinkets to encourage you—big good-luck charms from the hearts of the ones who will always love you. We're praying for you, and we believe your baby is going to have a future as bright and lovely as your past. Love, Mom, Dad, and Mitchell*
> *P.S. Mitchell says to take care of the Hotwheels. They could be worth something on E-bay!*

Sidney laughed as she put the treasures back in the box and set it on the floor. She laid on the bed and looked at the antique white ceiling, remembering the glow-in-the-dark constellation that had been there when she made wishes on the invisible North Star.

Chapter Fourteen

IT WAS A long flight home. Peter held her hand briefly a couple of times, but Alexis still felt betrayed. She had won him, true, but she wasn't sure he was a prize she wanted to keep. He was like one of those silly children's meal toys that seem cheap and useless but people somehow end up collecting. She knew she had to try, because somewhere under the plastic fragility there might be something valuable to hang on to.

Kristen had been so patient through this mess that had taken over her peaceful home. They could count on her to keep their secret until Alexis could decide what to do and how to feel about it.

Alexis knew she should feel excited about her new secret, but it seemed impossible after all that had happened. She worried that she would look like a fool. On the other hand, if anyone had the right to carry his child it was his wife! She should have suspected something; she had been feeling the same as she had before. She was feeling tired and emotional lately, but who wouldn't be, given her circumstances? Those feelings could have been caused by the stress. The heartbreak could have robbed her of energy. She had excuses for everything. Well, everything except the problem with the toothpaste. The smell and the taste turned her stomach and landed her on her knees in front of the toilet bowl.

Kristen had been suspicious. "Have you had your period yet?" she'd asked one morning.

"I'm late," Alexis answered, "but I'm sure it's just stress. I'll get back on track when my life straightens out."

Kristen nodded, but clearly had her own opinions. The next morning she laid a home pregnancy test on the counter in the bathroom with a sticky note attached that said, *Humor me.*

Alexis had been annoyed, but she did as her sister asked, thinking of it as more a waste of money than a prediction of things to come. In fact, she'd even thrown the stick away before looking at it, feeling stupid for entertaining the idea. Babies were a product of love, and Peter's love had been with someone else. It wasn't possible.

She might have believed it if she'd kept her eyes away from the wastebasket, away from that stupid life-changing stick that was infuriating her and calling her to it. *Positive!* That's what it said. Was it positive to be pregnant at the same time as her husband's mistress? She felt sick and confused.

"Maybe it's not as bad as you think." Kristen had attempted to encourage her. "Maybe it will drive home to Peter what he may have lost."

"I want him to be with me because he wants to be, not because he feels obligated. Peter was a great father, and I know he can be again, but I need more than that. I need a faithful husband who loves me and thinks about me."

Kristen wouldn't let it drop. There was a niece or nephew on the way, whether his or her parents stayed together not. She would be excited about it if even if no one else was.

Alexis wasn't looking at him, and Peter noticed she'd been avoiding him. He realized that his confession and apology didn't guarantee her forgiveness. He'd ripped a hole in her heart that only trust could mend. He would have to earn that trust.

Peter wondered how long he would feel ashamed, irresponsible, and selfish. He hated himself; he always had. His pride was a mask to cover up how weak he felt. He felt buried under the weight of it. He had to change, to earn a second chance to accomplish the impossible—Alexis' forgiveness and his own. How long would he run from the grief? How long would he hate the color pink? Lingerie? All the things he blamed for his bad decisions.

There had been a time early in their marriage when Alexis had worn silk and satin that caused his senses to tingle. It hadn't been because of a lack of effort or interest when she pulled on one of his old T-shirts. What that really said was that she felt secure. They didn't need frills. He had foolishly misread and resented it. He had become bored and disappointed and was ashamed to tell her. As she had snuggled in, cozy and secure, he had withdrawn—unsure and insecure.

She looked out the window as they flew through the night. He glanced at her and thought he saw a hint of hope in her face. Was it for them? Could she forgive what he'd done? Was there a chance? He closed his eyes, rested, and prayed silently until touchdown, wondering if God even listened to men like him.

There was a stack of mail on the kitchen counter, mostly junk and a few bills. The cat rubbed himself against their legs and made it almost impossible for them to get in the house. The air was humid and smelled stale. Alexis hated that smell. She lit a candle first thing. Peter dodged the cat and headed down the hall with their bags banging against his legs.

Alexis looked around at the mess she'd abandoned—dishes still in the dishwasher, wedding pictures turned over in the frames. She'd been angry, and there was a broken orange juice glass on the kitchen floor to remind her. She hadn't thrown it at Peter; he hadn't even been there. But he'd been in her head when she packed her things.

How could she bring a child here? Raise a child here? It seemed hostile and silent, not at all ideal. But their life never had been perfect. There had always been something more that seemed just beyond their reach—something wonderful that they couldn't quite seem to grab.

Then there was Zeek. He was a perfect baby, a perfect child. Something beautiful they had attained together. Then their dream of his future had slipped through their hands like sand.

"Ashes to ashes, dust to dust." If he was in the ashes she would light a fire every night and look for his face in the flame. If he was dust she would run her fingers over her dusty window pane and imagine the feel of his baby-soft skin. But there was an emptiness that ashes and dust couldn't fill.

She wouldn't be alone, though. Within her there was someone—a life. Still, her loneliness seemed permanent. When would she tell Peter? *How* would she tell him?

For now, she just wanted a little peace.

Chapter Fifteen

NICKY COULDN'T SHAKE the tune and lyrics of "Hush Little Baby" from her head. Who knew that lullaby could become a ring tone for a cell phone? The smile on Jennifer's face every time it rang was bigger and brighter than Nicky could have imagined.

Brad was excited. In one week the guest room was transformed into a beautiful, whimsical nursery that made both Nicky and Jennifer cry. Nicky slept surrounded by baby paraphernalia, feeling and thinking things she'd never thought or felt before. She had never expected to feel such jealousy. Not just of Jennifer but of the baby that was stealing away her friends' thoughts and emotions. Jennifer was a mother now. She didn't need to see the baby to know that she was going to have everything she'd ever wanted. She could breathe again, even relax a little.

But Nicky was feeling restless, afraid, and uncertain. She too felt like a mother, living unselfishly and deeper than ever before. But this couldn't be put into words. It felt foolish, even in her private thoughts.

It hadn't been easy, and it certainly wasn't painless, but the result was a new life. The goal had been achieved.

Nicky couldn't explain her feelings and didn't know how to give it words. She felt fragile, constantly worried for the little life inside her. They were inseparable now, she and the baby. They were as bonded as she and Jennifer had been long ago, back when everything seemed easy.

The old song was a lie, really, or at least a false hope: First comes love, then comes marriage, then comes a baby in a baby carriage. It wasn't always true. There were many carriages that held the babies of unwed mothers, and many brokenhearted men and women who would never push a baby carriage. Love doesn't have a pattern, and it doesn't follow reason. It makes its own way, pushing through obstacles and indifference, refusing to fade or give up on what might be.

Now, looking back, even Nicky's own dreams had seemed so simple before she knew what it took to make a successful life. There had been hours of study in history, art, and anthropology as she prepared to pursue her dream. She had loved the trips to the museum with her mother, but as a child she had lacked the realization of what it had taken for her mother to achieve such a prestigious position there. All she knew was that the same hand that held hers as she crossed the street had also repaired tapestries that had belonged to royalty. It had fascinated her, the way those simple mommy hands had taken such elaborate care to restore the beauty of another's creation.

Nicky hadn't realized dreams had so many layers. She was a child then, and it was easy to say, "I want to be like my mom." Funny, she never thought of being a mom, just being like *her* mom. When had everything changed? When had it gone from a simply-stated dream to an overwhelmingly distant reality? Things had changed. She was amazed at how quickly the guestroom was transformed. Even the lemony scent in the sheets had been replaced by something like baby powder. Everything was different—clean and new. Even her.

It was Sunday when she began to feel a bit normal again. It was more than just her body that needed recovery time, it was her soul. There was a mental battle to find herself again, to see her identity in this foreign experience. She had lost everything familiar and predictable about her own life, even her home. She was starting over.

The knock on the bedroom door signaled that Jennifer was done in the bathroom and the shower was available. Nicky looked at the dress lying on the bed, the one she and Jennifer had found on a recent shopping trip. Was she becoming a princess too? The dress was so feminine, so simple and casual. It screamed "church dress."

She carried the clothes into the bathroom and turned on the water. Her body didn't feel different yet, but she felt differently about her body. She ran her fingers over her stomach as if there were something to feel. Was the water too hot for the baby? She had never wondered or worried about another person so much, but she tilted the nozzle slightly to the left and let the water cool down. It was important. There was someone more important than herself.

"You look nice," Jennifer told her as she poured them both some orange juice.

"I don't look like a teacher?" Nicky asked.

"Absolutely not," Brad assured her. His cologne filled the kitchen. It was thick and spicy. Nicky tried to breathe through her mouth, eager for the fragrance to disappear under the aroma of percolating coffee. Once the coffeemaker filled the pot it was quickly removed and unplugged. The steaming liquid was poured into two insulated coffee mugs for the ones who could indulge in caffeine as much as they wished.

Nicky felt strange as they entered the church foyer. She searched the walls for some religious symbolism but saw only bare walls; concrete blocks painted white, and signs directing them to restrooms and classrooms and other destinations. It was basic minimalism, humble and unpretentious.

She followed Jennifer down a long hallway, past a line where parents were checking in infants and uneasy toddlers. She studied the scene as they passed, captured by the flexibility of the infants being passed from adult to adult. They didn't seem fazed at all by whose arms held them, as long as they were held.

The parents appeared anxious about the transfer, however. A mommy stood frozen, expecting a squeal of discomfort to escape from her infant's lips, before walking away robotically, suddenly made awkward by empty arms that now knew only how to hold that child. The babies didn't seem to care.

Is that how it would feel for her in February when she would lay a baby in her friend's arms and surrender the feeling of motherhood to her? Would this baby be as indifferent, or would it cry out for the one who had carried it?

She shook off the thought and followed Jennifer into the colorful children's church. It was strange to be in a church, but even stranger to be seated in a red folding chair next to a smiling eight-year-old.

Jennifer was a leader in the children's department and Brad worked the soundboard. The kids obviously loved them. The service opened with prayer by the children's pastor and live music that encouraged children to jump like frogs and flap their arms like birds. She laughed at Jennifer jumping in her high heels and waving her arms like a duck headed south. It was good to see such joy on her friend's face. She was amazed by how easily Jennifer shed the reserved ladylike image to be silly and unashamed.

Before long, Nicky found herself jumping up and down alongside an eight-year-old admirer. The pastor spoke about surrendering everything to God. He spoke kid lingo as he told them the story about the rich young ruler who didn't want to give up what he had in order to follow Christ.

"Let it go," he said. "Give it up and follow Jesus.

There was a puppet skit and a game. He called out a boy and a girl from the crowd and gave them each a pack of McDonald's gift certificates. He told them they could keep what they'd been given and sit down, or they could give the prize to a friend who would enjoy it. Both children were willing to give away their prize, and the pastor led them to a side room where he gave them each another pack of gift certificates and a twenty-dollar bill.

"Letting go of what you have is never easy," he told them. "It's a risk that may be rewarded here on earth or may not be until you reach heaven. No matter what, it's always worth it when you give up your best to find God's best for you."

Nicky had given herself up for her friends. She remembered the nurse at the clinic telling her that she was "laying her life down for a friend." It hadn't been easy to give it up or let it go, but she had done it. She had emptied herself, that much was true, but she was feeling the loss. There was something missing, and in her heart she understood. It was time to follow God empty-handed and vulnerable. She didn't have to have a plan anymore, she only had to follow.

As the lights dimmed and the children bowed their heads for the closing prayer, she found herself repeating that man's prayer silently. What happened next wasn't important anymore. She didn't have to be a step ahead because God knew what her future held, and for the first time ever, that was enough.

Chapter Sixteen

IT WAS BRAD and Jennifer's first night out together, just the two of them, since Nicky's arrival. They had been concerned about her and hadn't wanted to leave her alone. The medications she had been on caused her to feel emotional and tired. The doctor had explained that Nicky's emotions following the procedure would be similar to those of a cancer patient. But it seemed she was beginning to feel better now. She was resting more and was becoming more open with them about her feelings. Brad and Jennifer needed this evening together. Truth be told, Jennifer had been so wrapped up in caring for Nicky that she had started neglecting Brad a little.

Jennifer swished the powdered blush across her cheek bones, giving special care to the pressure she applied. She was wearing a simple black dress, and her hair was down. Brad loved her long hair and always complained when she wore it up. She applied pink lip gloss before flipping off the light and rushing down the stairs.

Nicky looked up as Jennifer came into the room. "You either need to teach him how much cologne is appropriate or I'm buying him a different brand."

"Where is he?" Jennifer asked.

"Just follow the trail of nausea," Nicky laughed. "I think he's outside with the pooch."

Jennifer found him outside, tossing a ball for the dog to fetch.

"You ready, babe?" he asked, pulling the ball out of Georgie's mouth as he led her inside. He had planned their date himself, telling Jennifer only that she should dress up a little.

He opened the car door for her, eyeing her legs as she slid in. She had perfect legs, slender and muscular.

"We have some rules tonight," he said as they pulled out of the driveway. "First, we will not talk about Nicky or the baby. Tonight is about us. Okay?"

Jennifer nodded.

"Second, you have to relax and have fun. Promise?"

"I promise. Where are you taking me?"

He smiled but didn't answer as he pushed in a CD.

"What is this?" she laughed. "Is that the old mix CD I gave you when we started dating?"

"Bringing back memories?"

Brad pulled into the parking lot of the old diner that had once been owned by Brad's uncle. It was where they had come on their first date.

"You had me dress up to eat here?" she asked, trying not to sound disappointed.

"Now, Princess, give me a chance. This is only phase one." They walked into the diner and were escorted to the booth they had shared on their first date. The hostess who led the way was wearing blue-checkered high tops. She quickly removed the "reserved" sign handwritten on yellow note paper and stuck to the end of the table by transparent tape.

Brad ordered for them both. "Two old-fashioned, open-face turkey sandwiches, please, one with mashed potatoes and one with a baked potato and sour cream on the side. We'd like two chocolate malts and a glass of water for each of us."

He turned his attention to Jennifer. "Isn't it amazing what God has done for us? It wasn't that long ago when we would come here and talk about our dreams. Remember when my uncle was selling this place and I was a wreck because I wanted to buy it but we didn't have the funds? Now we own a beautiful restaurant that pulls in triple what this place earns, and Taste of Ohio calls it a top dining experience. It's nuts, really."

"How's work been lately?" It was the first time she had asked about business for nearly a month.

That was just the question he'd been hoping she would ask when he started the conversation.

"You aren't going to believe this, but we served a food critic last week without knowing it. He is traveling across America looking for restaurants with the best vegetable dishes."

"We don't have vegetarian entrees," Jennifer interrupted.

"Well, we didn't," Brad said. "But I'd been playing with the portabella ravioli a little, and it's actually a fully vegetarian dish now. The ravioli is made with a sweet potato batter and packed with diced vegetables and covered in the portabella sauce. Anyway, he loved it. He wants to write about us in his book!"

"Honey, that's great!"

"That's not all. He's going to be interviewed on a few talk shows where guests and the host will sample some of the dishes he mentions in his book. He wants to know if I'll make an appearance for him. Do you know how much business this could earn for us?"

Jennifer picked at her sandwich, suddenly hungry for her husband's new dish. She smiled at him, thrilled with his latest success. He was so handsome when he felt confident.

They sat and talked for a long time, discussing Brad's opportunity and the upcoming enrollment drive for her dance studio in early August. Classes would begin in September and the whirlwind of preparing young dancers for the studio performance of *The Nutcracker* would begin in earnest.

When their plates were empty and the last drops of malt fished out with long spoons, phase two of their date began. Walking out into the night, Jennifer discovered there was a carriage waiting for them, pulled by two white horses.

Brad helped her into the seat and presented her with a bouquet of roses.

"Don't design your tiara just yet. You don't know where I'm taking you," Brad teased.

"I love you," Jennifer whispered, resting her head against his chest.

They held hands as the carriage clipped along before coming to a stop in front of Mr. Hensley's bike shop. Brad lifted her from the carriage, enjoying her surprise. He led her around to the back of the old shop.

"Why are we here?" This was the spot where they had nearly ended their engagement. They'd been on their way back from getting ice cream when they began to bicker about something she couldn't even remember. They were both nervous about the future and were masking their fear with unplanned words and high emotions. They almost gave up on each other and walked away from their future together right here behind Hensley's bike shop.

"What do you think now? Do you think it was worth the risk?"

"That was a terrible night. I'm sorry it ever happened," she answered quietly.

"I'm not! I learned then that you're the one for me. You always will be."

They walked back to the carriage and rode to the diner and their car. He drove her to the studio and had her use her key to open the door. Marcy, her fellow teacher, had left candles and matches right where he asked her to. He carried them into the back studio and lined them up and lit them. He set up the CD player with the volume low and pulled Jennifer against him, and they danced with the candles flickering yellow in the mirrors.

They kissed as they rocked together until the rocking stopped and they were just a man and a woman backed together in a loving embrace. They stayed at the studio late into the night on a blanket Brad had brought from home. They talked about everything between kisses and tender glances, and as the night unfolded they talked about the baby as well. God had blessed them again and again. A baby! Could their hearts hold so much love? They agreed that they could. They knew they loved each other more now than they'd ever thought possible. Surely their hearts could grow again.

Chapter Seventeen

THE FIRST TIME Kristen dialed Joey's number she couldn't help but think what her mother would say. Some of the teachings from her childhood had left an indelible mark. The point had been driven home hard and often that girls do not call boys. It isn't ladylike!

It had been so ingrained in her that it had become a ridiculous problem in adulthood. There was just something about hearing a male voice on the other end of the phone that felt naughty, whether it was Peter answering for Alexis or her dad or the pizza guy.

She knew Joey couldn't call her, even if he wanted to. She hadn't given him her number, but he had scribbled down his number for her.

He answered on the fourth ring. There was a click of an answering machine turning off and a breathless, "Hello? Are you there?"

"I'm here. It's Kristen. You're out of breath. Did I call at a bad time?"

"No, not at all. I was just getting out of the shower."

"I can call back," she said quickly.

"Why? I'm dressed. It's all good." He laughed. "So, what's up? You calling to set up a one-on-one rematch?"

"Nothing's up, really. I was just surprised after our lunch the other day. I never knew you to be a religious person, and now you want to see if you've still got it on the court? Besides, I don't have a ball, and you just got out of the shower, remember?"

"Oh, so you're afraid of losing, huh?" he taunted.

Kristen could say no to the dare, but she didn't really want to. Half an hour later she was turning into his apartment complex to play the sport she hadn't played in years. He met her at the sidewalk with the basketball hugged under his arm. He passed her the ball and she carried it onto the court. The touch and smell of the ball soothed her like an old friend. She'd almost forgotten the feel of the bubbled surface and tight firmness, the rubbery athletic smell. She hadn't realized how much she missed it.

"You better watch yourself," she warned as she made a shot at the basket. "It's all coming back."

They played hard, each dribble on the asphalt spurring them on. Joey tried to block her, but she stayed low and moved fast. Her wrists remembered how to land the ball perfectly inside the red rim.

"Are you sure you haven't played since high school?" he asked after losing.

"Are you sure you *have*?" she teased.

They sat together on a green bench next to the court drinking the sports drinks he had brought. They talked quietly as they cooled off and their heart rates returned to normal. Kristen looked at Joey in the shadows under the light post. He'd become a man, but she could still see the boy she had known so long ago, even though his face now showed evidence of a beard and his shoulders had become broader and more muscular.

As Kristen drove home, she wondered where this was headed. Was Joey the answer to that quiet prayer only she and God knew about? Women weren't supposed to need men anymore in this new millennium. Women had their own opportunities and were self-sufficient. It was insulting for society to assume that all single women pine for husbands. Life could be lived and enjoyed without a diamond on that all-important finger.

And it was almost true for Kristen. She could be happy without being married. She certainly didn't need a man to validate her existence or make her feel good about herself. She was too smart for that. But she still believed that the love of a man could enhance her life. She liked the idea of having a partner—a teammate to pass the ball to when she knew she couldn't make the basket. She had prayed for it in secret, exposing her loneliness only to God. She knew God had heard her, just as he'd heard every other prayer, whether it was a silent prayer from her heart or spoken out loud.

Could it be that a door was opening and her life would soon be moving at a faster pace with love front and center?

Chapter Eighteen

THE ROOM WAS green, and there were ivy and fern plants in every corner. An aloe plant sat on the edge of the counselor's desk. Peter and Alexis sat side-by-side on the fluffy white sofa. The close physical proximity felt forced and unfamiliar.

Peter's elbow brushed against hers, and Alexis wondered if her flinching response was noticeable to anyone but herself. They were two separate individuals fighting to be heard, even understood. It didn't feel as if they belonged to each other.

"Alexis and I have spoken, as you know," the counselor began, addressing Peter. "She has something she needs to share with you and has asked that it be shared in the safety of this room."

Peter nodded nervously, and the counselor pointed her pen at Alexis, encouraging her to begin speaking.

It had to be told. She'd been amazed that he hadn't figured it out on his own. After all, she was beginning to show. It hurt that he hadn't noticed, and she wondered if he even looked at her anymore.

There was a pained expression in his eyes as he waited to hear her confession. She wondered if her news would soften that pain or if his fear would grow visibly.

"I'm pregnant," Alexis said. Her eyes were locked on his.

Peter pressed himself back into the cushions of the sofa, head cocked to one side. He was quiet, speechless in a way he'd never been before. Was the baby his? Would asking enrage her? He couldn't help himself, and the question flew out like a dart. "Is it mine?"

"Yes, it's yours!" Alexis stormed. "I was faithful, even when I knew you weren't! I've already seen the doctor a few times; I even heard the heartbeat. I'm showing, Peter. How could you be surprised?"

"When?" he asked, searching his memory for the last time they'd been intimate. It had to be some time back in March. Could she be that far along without him knowing?

"I'm due December fourth."

She was almost five months. He could see it now. Had he not noticed because he didn't want to?

Alexis handed him an ultrasound picture, and he stared at the face. It wasn't a mere caterpillar-gray shape in the center of a black triangle. It was a baby, tiny nose, sealed eyelids, a tiny chin, and part of him.

His betrayal felt deeper now, and he hung his head at the realization. He had left his pregnant wife to take another woman to the opera. He had not only risked his marriage, he had risked losing his family.

"How do you feel about this?" the counselor asked them both.

"I'm embarrassed," Alexis admitted. "It makes me feel foolish. Everyone will know that I trusted my husband—made love to him—when he was being unfaithful to me. I already love this baby though, and I want it."

"I'm embarrassed too," Peter answered. "But for completely different reasons. This makes what I did even worse. I don't know if I can ever make things right. This is unforgivable. It's never going to be a private thing that happened in our past. The other baby is going to be on the outskirts of my family, you know? I won't have to face that baby every day. I can love it at a distance. But this baby—how will I ever explain it? He or she is not going to miss the fact that there's a half brother or sister who is so close in age."

"I'm not looking for this baby to be a miracle cure for our marriage, Peter." Alexis looked intensely into his eyes. "I don't expect it to change things between us, and I don't want that kind of pressure to be on a baby. I just want you to see my commitment to fixing all the garbage between us. I want this baby, and I want to repair our marriage as well. I hope that it's not too much to ask."

Alexis felt even more awkward as their session ended and they walked out to the car.

There was a strange sense of relief. She allowed herself to comb her fingers over her belly. She wouldn't even rest her hand there for a moment before she told him. She'd held her breath too, sucking in her stomach in hopes of disguising the life it contained. She was breathing freely now, relieved that she no longer had anything to hide. The relaxation made her feel pregnant, as if her body suddenly had permission to be as it was.

"Have you scheduled your next appointment with the doctor?" Peter asked, his eyes never leaving the road.

"Yeah, it's scheduled. Would you like to come with me?" she offered hesitantly.

Peter nodded. "I think it's going to be good," he said. He smiled at her, a smile that told her he was in this with her. "When did you find out?"

She told him about the test, how she had fought taking it and hated even looking at it once she had. She told him how lonely she had been and how sneaky she felt going to the doctor's office when he thought she was out running errands. She told him about the night she had taken out Zeek's baby blanket and rocked it while he took a shower in the next room. She admitted her anxiety about continuing their family without their son. She said it felt like they would all be taking a trip somewhere great like Disney World and they'd left Zeek behind in a dingy hospital room with a picture of Mickey Mouse hanging over the bed. Zeek was their family too, and she wanted him back.

"Do you remember when we found out you were pregnant with him?" Peter asked.

"I'll never forget it," she answered. Her emotions were so different then. They were so happy, so amazed that their love had created something so meaningful. Was this baby a product of love or just an attempt at fulfilling a marital obligation? It didn't feel the same, and it made her sad.

The leaves were just beginning to fall from the trees in September when they went to the doctor together. Peter was adjusting to his new role at the school, teaching history and art. His students were no longer young adults only looking to meet credit requirements; he now taught awkward-looking twelve-year-olds at the middle school five minutes from his house. It had meant a cut in pay, but he felt fulfilled. He loved his life again, and he embraced all its changes.

Alexis arrived first and sat waiting for him. She turned her head toward the door as it opened. Peter took a seat beside her on a red-cushioned loveseat, rubbing his thumb against the back of her hand in a soft, loving motion until her name was called.

They had come a long way in just a month. It felt safe to touch each other again. Slowly, there was a sense of belonging growing between them that had been absent for a long time.

The midwife shook Peter's hand. She had delivered Zeek, though she had looked very different then. Peter supposed the years had changed them all.

Alexis slid up her sleeve so the blood pressure cuff could be wrapped around her arm. She stepped onto the scale, and her weight was recorded on the chart. Next, her stomach was measured. Then came the part Peter had come for.

Blue jelly was squirted on Alexis's stomach, and the midwife turned on the tiny gadget that quickly made the baby's heartbeat audible.

Peter stood holding Alexis's hand, trying to disguise the tears filling his eyes. There was a tiny heart in there, beating rapidly. He silently promised to never break that tiny heart. This baby might not have been conceived in love or passion, but he would love this child. More importantly, he would love its mother.

Chapter Nineteen

SIDNEY STOOD SILENTLY looking out the back door. She had never realized a backyard could tell such a story. The tufts of grass, the pattern of bark ripped off the lower part of the tree, and the chipped paint on the old wooden swing were the marks of her childhood. One couldn't guess it now, but there had been a terrific tree house back against the fence that separated their yard from the Parkers'. She could see it in her mind as if it still existed, a ghost in the north corner of the yard. She remembered crying when that old tree was taken out. It didn't matter that she was now in her twenties and no longer lived here. That tree house had been a sanctuary during the ups and downs of her teen years. It was the place where she could cry and not be seen. She worked through her life in that tree. Problems were simpler then, but at the time they were as monumental as any of her current problems.

It was a chilly morning, a perfect match for the hot herbal tea and warm cinnamon roll she carried outside with her. She rocked the old swing slowly, sipping the tea and staring at the empty corner where answers were once found.

The back door opened and her brother banged his way outside, balancing two bags of garbage. After putting them into the garbage can he joined her on the swing.

"You okay?" he asked as his foot stopped the rocking.

"Yeah, just kind of thinking, I guess." She gazed at the empty spot.

He followed her eyes and laughed. "Still upset about Fort Flannery?" Mitchell was teasing her, but for a moment they both saw the invisible. "What's wrong with you? Really? You look sad, and you're acting like you have a secret."

"Maybe I do," she whispered.

"Care to share?"

"Not particularly." She pushed her foot off the ground to resume the rocking.

"Okay. I'll start your confession for you." He looked up at the windows first. If Mom was watching he'd better not continue. He had learned early on that she could lip read better than any middle school girl they'd ever known. The coast was clear, so he continued.

"The 'donor' is no more anonymous than I am invisible."

Sidney stood up, amazed at his conclusion and the absolute certainty of it.

"Who is he?" Mitchell asked.

"How would you know that?" She scanned her memory for every lie she'd told, wondering where the flaw occurred.

"First of all, do you not remember who used to keep the window open in your room so you could get back in after sneaking out? Sorry, sis, but honesty hasn't been your strongest trait. Secondly, we're talking about *you*. You wouldn't start a family with a number, you'd want the man. However, it didn't dispute my theory to hear the guy in the background during a phone conversation a while back."

"Oh." She sat down on the swing again.

"So how long has he been married?"

"What makes you think—"

"Did you bring him home to meet the family?"

"Well, no."

"Did you tell Mom and Dad you were dating anyone?"

"No, but—"

"But we've already established that I see through this lie. How far do you plan to take it, Sid? Can you look me in the eye and tell me there's not some married dude involved in this?" He shook his head. "I'm not stupid, and neither is Mom."

"Mom knows?" Sidney's eyes bulged.

"I'm just saying she's not stupid," Mitchell answered.

"And Dad's no dummy, either. But he is always a little behind when it comes to me," Sidney responded.

"You want me to say it, okay. You're his favorite. You know it. I know it, I'm over it. Now tell me who this dude is and why you're lying to your family to protect him," Mitchell demanded.

"I'm not protecting him," Sidney protested.

"What then?" Mitchell shrugged.

"I'm protecting myself. How do you think they'd feel if they knew what I've done?"

"They'd be disappointed," he answered.

"Yeah." She rolled her eyes and nodded at the understatement.

"But they'd pray for you, Sid. Prayer is bigger than you can imagine. The kind of prayers you need right now. Guess what, they've never loved you because you're perfect. You never have been. They just love you."

"But this is big."

"No joke! But so is their love. I mean, don't expect them to invite the jerk for dinner, but they're not going to disown you or anything."

"Probably not," Sidney admitted.

"You want an answer, Sid. I'll give you one. Be honest. Trust us to love you enough anyway."

He left her there on the swing, kissing the top of her head before going back to the house.

She wished she could go back in time and take all the guilt with her. Why had she let her life get to this? She knew better.

Her mother was baking zucchini bread when she went back into the kitchen. Mom never sat still. She was Mrs. Cleaver on steroids. Sidney sat down at the kitchen counter and watched the batter spin around the heavy whipping blades. She didn't know how to say what needed to be said as she watched her mother clicking the button to increase the mixer's speed. Her shoulders sank under the shame of her secret, and the mixing came to an abrupt stop as Mom noticed her tears. The room was quiet as Mrs. Flannery sat down. Concern washed over her face and forced her wrinkles out of their hiding places. It was rare for her to sit this still.

"Why are you crying, baby?" Her voice was so soft Sidney barely heard her. "You can talk to me."

Something about the word *baby* made Sidney feel small, vulnerable, in need of her mother.

"Tell me," her mother coaxed.

"I'll disappoint you."

"I'll still love you," she insisted.

"It's about the baby." Sidney looked up at the windowsill with the tiny bird figurine displayed there. She wanted to fly away and disappear. Her mother's face kept her in the present, freezing her like that figurine.

"I knew the father. We were in love."

Mrs. Flannery looked puzzled, but she said nothing and waited for Sidney to continue.

"He's married, Mom, and he's staying married. I feel stupid and confused and afraid that I can't do this alone."

She could see the questions in her mother's eyes, but her silence gave Sidney courage.

"His name is Peter. We met at a party. He's a teacher. I didn't know he was married. I didn't even ask. Once I found out, I didn't know what to do. I convinced myself that he was in love with me and that I was the one he wanted to be with."

"You lied to us."

"Yes, I did." There, it was out in the open. "I thought it would hurt you less."

"You thought it would be easier," Mrs. Flannery corrected, resting her fingers against her temple and leaving a trail of flour in her hair.

"Yeah, I guess so," Sidney admitted. "I was afraid and ashamed and, yeah, it was easier to lie. I thought it would be better in the long run."

"Because you thought I wouldn't understand, right?"

"I didn't know."

"Do you consider it a mistake?" Mrs. Flannery asked. "I'm not talking about the baby. I'm talking about how you made a mistake with that man."

"Yes," Sidney answered.

"Honey, it *was* a mistake. A huge and hurtful mistake. It was selfish, and I am disappointed." She slid her fingers onto her daughter's neck and began to rub into her tension as she continued. "There have been times in my life that I have let people down, let God down. I've made mistakes too. Where do you think you got your mischievous side? It certainly wasn't from your father. That man doesn't even entertain the thought of running a stop sign, even when I was in labor with Mitchell. He follows the rules, and I like to test them. I guess you do too. You can say you're sorry, talk to God about it even, but you still have a fine to pay. That baby of yours is still coming and it's going to count on you, and you have to live up to that."

Sidney felt defeated. "I don't know how."

Mrs. Flannery laughed—a soft, muffled laugh. "You'll learn. It takes time to kill the flesh, honey. It's kind of like those candles your father used to put on Mitchell's cake—the ones that relight when you think they're out. You've got to keep huffing and puffing and maybe even use the help of water before it's over, but eventually it's over, and that candle can't be lit even if you try."

Sidney was amazed at her mother's ability to make illustrations out of the simplest things.

"You don't know everything about me, honey. You don't know all the ways your own mom has failed."

She started the mixer again and it began to punch the ingredients in the bowl as Mrs. Flannery returned to her baking. Sidney sat there watching her imperfect mother, wondering how long it would be before Daddy found out.

Chapter Twenty

BY OCTOBER NICKY was certain she had made the wrong decision. Surely there could have been another way that didn't involve her having sore feet and morning sickness. Poor Brad had been unable to cook pasta for the last four months. He didn't know what to do with himself. The smell of cooking tomatoes sent her stomach into fits of protest. She didn't want to eat anything except zucchini bread doused in canned frosting or cinnamon toaster pastries. Jennifer was quietly adamant that such foods were not sources of nutrition. She consistently nagged and pestered Nicky until she agreed to eat something with protein.

Good-bye size five. I'll miss you and all the lovely fashion styles you and I loved, she thought.

Nicky felt unpredictable and vulnerable and more unsure of herself than ever before. She had started walking to get some exercise, but that also had a lot to do with escaping the house.

A simple walk through the neighborhood exposed extreme differences in her life and Jennifer's. It forced her to see how little they had in common any longer. These houses were enormous, newly constructed homes that boasted several tall windows and walkways lined with greenery. A long way from Nicky's modest $500-a-month apartment.

She missed the simplicity of her life. Sure, there were a few plumbing issues, and the screen door leading to her balcony jammed occasionally, but it was home. It was what she was used to. It was familiar.

There were real trees in her apartment complex instead of baby trees not much bigger than sticks. These pathetic twigs were so weak they had to be held up by stakes on either side. Nicky wondered if she was a stake tied to the tree of Brad and Jennifer. Would they outgrow her once the baby came, once they became full and complete? They were growing their family tree, and she was carrying their dream until they could carry it themselves.

She was living in Jennifer's world now, wrapped so tightly into it that she felt she had no existence apart from it; no life of her own. With each kick to her side this baby seemed to be dissolving every shred of independence she had ever known. She was fading into a dream that belonged to someone else.

The gold-colored minivan pulled alongside her, the window rolled down.

"You shouldn't be walking this far," Jennifer reprimanded. "Climb in. I'll give you a ride."

"I'm fine," Nicky answered, waving her on. She wasn't in the mood to be babied. She couldn't deal with the smothering that was threatening their friendship.

"No you aren't. Get in," Jennifer insisted.

Nicky walked to the window. Jennifer smiled at her presumed control.

"I am carrying your child, Jennifer. I am not your child. I am walking. The doctor says it's good for me, and it's what I want to do. Go home and allow me the only opportunity I have for privacy these days."

Jennifer said nothing. Her eyebrows rose as Nicky backed away from the window and started to jog.

God, why couldn't she have her own baby? Why did she have to need me? This is too hard. She slowed to a brisk walk. *God, I'm not strong enough. I hate that I'm not strong enough.*

She was talking to God a lot lately. He was a silent shoulder she could unload on without having to face human judgment or listen to self-serving advice. She truly mattered to Him. She couldn't explain how she knew it, but she knew it.

About ten minutes later she heard a car horn behind her. She clenched her jaw and her fists. She didn't want to be friends with a princess today. She wasn't up for bowing to royal commands. Her white flag of surrender was ripped up and thrown away. She didn't want to surrender anymore. But she couldn't help but turn her head toward the sound of the horn. The minivan pulled alongside her again. Brad was at the wheel this time. Great! Reinforcements.

"For crying out loud! I just want to go for a walk!" Nicky whined, her ponytail bouncing.

"Okay," Brad answered.

"Okay?" Nicky knew it couldn't be that easy.

"Let's go for a walk."

She waited as he parked on the street and got out of the car. Despite the tinted windows, she caught him in a smirk.

"What's so funny?" she demanded, her hands on her hips.

His hands flew up in surrender. "Hey, I'm just a guy, okay? Remember, we aren't supposed to understand this stuff." He laughed.

"What's to understand?"

"Hmmm. Where should I start? You're supposed to relax, and you're out here working up a sweat."

"I'm not sweating!"

"You're sweating. Meanwhile, my perfectly healthy wife is at home crying so hard she nearly threw up. Call me crazy, but I don't get it."

"She's so dramatic," Nicky said.

"Maybe."

"No, trust me, she's dramatic. All she has to do is wait, and she'll have everything she ever wanted. She just has to wait, and she doesn't even get what it's been like for me. I've stopped being a person for her, and she's whining because I want to take a walk."

"She's worried about you."

Nicky shook her head. "She's worried about her baby."

"She's worried about you both. She doesn't want to lose you in order to be a mom."

"Well, someone's got to walk the plank, right? Her life isn't big enough."

"Now who's dramatic?"

They walked in silence until Brad got up the courage to ask her what he wanted to know.

"What's going to happen when this is over? Are you going to be able to leave us and the baby and go back to life as you knew it?"

"I think that's what scares me most," Nicky answered. "How do I go back to my life as if I've just been on vacation or something? It's like time is frozen for me. I don't fit in my old life anymore. How do I start over with nothing?"

Brad grabbed her hand, pulling her back in the direction of the car.

"I have an idea. Come with me."

"But…"

"Walk's over. Come on."

She walked with him, curious about his absolute determination.

He helped her into the minivan and began to drive. He pulled to a stop in front of a beautiful old home.

"This house is for sale," he informed her.

"I can't afford a house like this!"

"I know that. But I can. The problem is I'm not an eligible buyer. This house is owned by the historical society. They can't afford to restore it on the city's budget, but they refuse to sell it to anyone who won't or can't bring it back to its original state. I wouldn't know where to start. The first map of the city was drawn up in this house. It wasn't on the Underground Railroad, but it was special. This house has history."

"What does that have to do with me?"

"Portabella's is ready to expand, branch out a little. And this home has the most fantastic dining room. Together, we could make it something again."

"You want to make it into a restaurant?"

"A formal place with loads of history and beauty. Perfect for weddings and banquets. Really classy affairs. You could live here. You know—maintain it and restore it."

"Wow. You've given this a lot of thought."

"I have. We don't want to lose you once the baby's born, and we don't want you to lose yourself either."

Nicky looked at the aged brick, the ivy climbing across the front, and the thatched cottage windows. It was beautiful.

She felt the baby kick or flutter, or maybe push.

"Go for it," it seemed to say to her.

Maybe they all needed her to stay, even wanted her to stay. Maybe she wouldn't have to say good-bye. She smiled as she rubbed her hand over her stomach.

"You're family, you know," Brad said as he watched her soften.

"I know." Suddenly she felt tired. "Can we go home?"

Brad smiled and nodded.

"Oh! And I didn't sweat!" Nicky laughed.

Chapter Twenty-One

THE COLD WEATHER might have ended everything between Joey and Kristen. It forced them into a new phase—brought an end to the safe basketball games they'd become accustomed to. Their one-on-one games usually ended with a peck or two on the winner's cheek or a playful squeeze. It was casual, a slow evolution from friendship to romance. They were becoming dates. She would dress up, and he would hold her hand. Their eyes were on each other, not the ball. They were having conversations, verbal intimacy, and they were learning about each other.

She was falling in love, and for the first time she saw her future differently. Maybe God did know her after all. Maybe her loneliness had been temporary, a time of preparation. It was strange how much this relationship was changing her. She could be alone now without feeling empty. She felt certain her aloneness wouldn't last forever, and that gave her the peace to relax and enjoy the quiet. She wasn't living in the space between solitude and fulfillment. She was secure and centered and patient and ready for whatever God was about to give her.

This was a perfect day, a Saturday of pure rest. She had been cozy under an afghan Alexis had crocheted years ago. She was in her pajamas and sipping tea when the telephone rang. It rang four times before she answered it, even though it was on the table right beside her. She wasn't rushing for anyone today.

"Hello?"

"Hi. I was starting to think you were out with Joey again." It was Alexis.

"Nope. Not today. What's going on?"

"I'm calling about Thanksgiving. Mom and Dad are coming to visit Peter and me. Mom wants to be here when the baby comes, and Dad's along for the ride. Anyway, we didn't want you to be alone, or isn't that an issue?"

"I'm dating Joey, not married to him. Yeah, I'd like to be with my family for Thanksgiving. Will you have room for me, or should I get a room somewhere?"

"Well, Mom and Dad will be sleeping in the guest room. We've turned the den into the nursery. You could sleep in the studio, but I've been doing a lot of pottery lately, and it kind of smells."

"So I should get a room."

"Yeah, probably." Alexis tried to disguise the relief.

Kristen knew she'd be exactly the same way if she had company this close to having a baby.

"We'll have a ton of food, so Joey's welcome if you want to bring him."

"You think I should ask him?" Kristen was unsure.

"Why not?"

"I don't know. Isn't it weird? We've not been together that long."

"Yes you have. You two just didn't realize it at first. That's Joey, though. He's the only guy I know who can take a girl out on a date and somehow avoid any and all dating clichés. He's so casual he wouldn't tell you he loved you even if he did."

"He's told me he loves me," Kristen confessed.

"Really?" Alexis couldn't hide her surprise "When? Why didn't you tell me?"

"It was last week. I'm not even sure he realized he said it."

"Trust me, he realized he said it! That guy plans out every word he says. I wish I could be like that. I open my mouth and stuff just flies out."

Maybe I should ask him to come with me, Kristen thought. *Maybe it's natural to ask. Maybe this is going faster than I expected.*

She thought about it all night. Would he think she was pushy? Did he know she was serious about him? She hadn't told him she loved him. She didn't want to acknowledge that he had said it because she was afraid he had misspoken. It was silly insecurity, really. Alexis was right about him. Everything he said was always deliberate. He'd waited for a random unromantic moment that wasn't muddled up with emotion. It was honest and pure, and it melded into their conversation as casually as his breathing. She had become a part of him, but she'd given him no response.

By Sunday morning she was a ball of nerves. *God, why am I like this? Why am I so afraid to be loved?*

She met Joey in the lobby of his church. He was talking to some of his buddies, but he left them when he saw her.

"You look beautiful," he said as he helped her take off her coat.

She smiled, knowing she'd been blessed with another compliment from the heart of Joey Bentley.

"I'm sorry I didn't respond to you, Joey, when you told me you loved me." She took a breath and began hanging her coat in the coat room. "The thing is… well… I love you too."

She was distracting herself, trying to say it as casually as he'd said it. Casual didn't work for Kristen, though, and as she turned to face him she knew it hadn't been enough.

"I'm in love with you, Joey Bentley. I am."

He smiled at her and took her hand. He knew how big her words were and how hard it had been for her to say them. What he didn't know was the acceleration of her heart. He didn't know she was going to invite him into her Thanksgiving tradition. It was perfect, after all. He was what she would give thanks for. He was her blessing, her answered prayer. Now all she had to do was ask.

Does Kristen drink Sprite or 7-up?" Mrs. McGowen asked from the kitchen.

"I can't remember," Alexis admitted. "I bought both to be safe."

The table was set, and the turkey was in the oven. Alexis made the cranberry-orange relish, and her mother made the mashed potatoes.

Mrs. McGowen's mashed potatoes were the highlight of family meals. She put cheese on top of the potatoes after they were mashed. Alexis had made her specialty, ambrosia salad, and Kristen was bringing her gourmet cheesecake. Kristen and Joey would be arriving with it shortly. It was going to be great having everyone together.

The house smelled delicious, rich and warm in every way. Alexis was so hungry she had a stomach ache. Her mother let her snitch a bite of the mashed miracle, but the aching continued.

"Are you feeling okay?" Peter asked as he watched her shifting her weight in discomfort.

"Are you having some Braxton Hicks contractions, maybe?" Mom suggested.

"Should we time them? Alexis, why don't you sit down?" Peter adjusted the cushions on the couch for her.

"Don't be silly," she laughed. "Dinner's almost ready, and Kristen will be here any minute. I don't need to lie down. I need to eat."

They heard a car door shut outside, and the men began moving the food to the dining room table. Alexis waited in the doorway and watched as Joey grabbed Kristen's hand and let her lead him up the walkway.

"Hello, Prego!" Joey teased. Alexis felt the baby balling up tightly, and she knew it was time to sit down.

This was more than hunger, and she wondered how much longer she could ignore it. She would be happy if she could just get through the meal.

She hugged her sister and took their coats. Just as she was about to turn, she felt a tug and a pop, and warm liquid dripped down her leg onto the hardwood floor.

They all stared at her, then at the beautifully set table, as if they regretted not being able to sit down and eat as much as she regretted it.

"We probably have time to eat before we go to the hospital." Alexis tried to sound convincing.

"You two get out of here! We'll package this up and be right behind you," Mom instructed Peter. She was already scooping food into

Tupperware containers, while Mr. McGowen carved the turkey in a practical manner, minus the glamour and precision he usually brought to the task.

Kristen mopped up the floor. Alexis changed her clothes, and Peter took their bags to the car.

In fifteen minutes they were and on their way. In twenty-five minutes their house was empty except for the aroma of a meal that comes only once a year.

The contractions were intense, and Peter could tell by her furrowed brow that it wouldn't be long. He'd forgotten that detail of Zeek's birth; the way she expressed her pain by lowering her eyebrows. He could tell the onset of a contraction by that simple bend of her brow.

She was a quiet laborer, focusing her pain inward and working her fears out in her mind. That was how it was last time. Somehow, everything was different now. She needed to be heard, to be alert, and focus outside herself. There was too much disappointment inward. She couldn't think or her mind would go to Zeek and the tiny casket they'd placed him in. She had to be strong; she had to forget at least for the moment.

She was admitted quickly, and the examination showed that it wouldn't be long until she delivered.

Four hours and eighteen minutes later, with Mrs. McGowen holding her left hand and Kristen holding her right hand, she gave the final push. Peter's eyes locked on hers, and the rest of the room disappeared as life poured out of her, stinging and burning and beautiful.

The baby was laid on her stomach. He was perfect. Ten fingers, ten toes, rich black hair. He was six pounds seven ounces and twenty inches long. He had Zeek's chin and cheeks, but he was very much his own person. An absolute blend of his parent's features.

"I love you," Peter said, kissing her head and pushing her hair from her face.

He held the baby's tiny hand and let the little fingers curl around his index finger.

Kristen and her mother left the room to tell her dad and Joey. Alexis and Peter and their son were a family, alone for the first time.

"I thought it would be a boy," Peter confessed.

"You did?"

"Yeah, it was just a feeling I had. I bought something for him a few weeks ago. A boy has to have a car." He held up a plush, stuffed car he had packed in secret. "His brother would be proud," Peter said quietly. "You did wonderful."

"We have to be better, Peter. We have to love each other more, laugh more. We have to give him a family." Alexis' eyes brimmed with hope and tears.

"I'm staying, Alexis, for you. Because you matter. I love you, and I'm sorry I ever forgot it. The baby is icing on the cake. Beautiful, so small and unexpected. I don't deserve either of you."

She held his hand as the nurse took the baby away to bathe him. They were new together, people changed and matured by the test they'd put each other through.

"What should we name him?" Alexis asked. "Do you still like Christian?"

"I think Christian Spencer Marks is our miracle in diapers," Peter answered.

They waited quietly for their clean baby to return, both silently wondering how Peter's other child would be born. They were trying not to wonder how different it would feel; trying to wall off the emotions that seemed too big for either of them.

Chapter Twenty-Two

"DO YOU THINK I'm hard to talk to?" Mrs. Flannery whispered to her husband. They were in bed, and she couldn't turn her mind off. It was playing back her conversation with Sidney, making her wonder and worry and reflect.

"No, but you are hard to hear," he teased. "Are you okay? You seem as if something is bothering you."

She shook her head in the dark and stared at the ceiling. It wasn't supposed to be like this. Where had things gone wrong?

Sidney had been in church since she was two weeks old until she was sixteen. It wasn't just church attendance, either. They had made God a welcome part of their family. They prayed together and did devotions twice a week. They had family Fridays when they ordered pizza and played board games together. It lasted for a while anyway. The teen years changed everything. Those years challenged all the beliefs they'd instilled in Sidney and caused her to question everything and redefine her life in a less-than-pleasing way.

"What is it?" He rolled onto his side to face her. He'd been married long enough to know not to ignore silences.

"I'm just thinking about Sidney," she confessed.

He squeezed her hand "I know, honey. I wish she had been married first too."

"It's not just that."

"I know. The baby's never going to know its daddy. What's she going to do, say that Daddy was just a number? It doesn't make any sense to me, either."

Mrs. Flannery turned her head. She hated having a secret between them. She couldn't tell him, so she told the wall and let him listen.

"She'll be able to give a name. Maybe the baby will even meet him—if his wife allows it."

He turned her chin to face him "What are you talking about?"

"She had an affair, honey. She lied to us."

"No. She knows better than to do a fool thing like that!"

"Yes, that's what I thought too. I'm so confused. We gave her to God. How did she forget everything we taught her?"

"She didn't, honey," he answered. "It's still there. Remember the Prodigal Son? She's hit bottom. We have to let her find her way back. She finally told you the truth; that's got to say something. Why do you think she didn't tell me?"

"I've been wondering that too. You two speak your own language. She's always gone to you. Maybe she thought I'd be less disappointed."

"I don't think so. Maybe she wanted something from you."

"Like what?" she asked.

"The truth. I would have frozen. I would have been so afraid of scaring her off, I probably would have sounded as if I approved. I bet you told her the truth. I bet you reminded her who she really let down."

"You think?"

"I do. Maybe she needs a little honesty. You should spend some time alone with her. Remind her that she belongs to God. Don't judge her or anything. Just be real."

It was quiet after that, and they both settled under the covers in the dark.

It had been a long time since she'd spent time alone with her daughter. There had been that day in the salon when Sidney was fifteen. It had been memorable, but not in a positive way. Sidney thought she would look great as a blonde. Her natural color was somewhere between a light brown and a dirty blonde. It didn't seem like too big a change until the process had been completed and the color was set.

"I look like I belong on Geraldo!" she had cried.

A better mother wouldn't have laughed at the thought of a mob mistress in wide sunglasses and a blonde wig four tones lighter than her skin. Unfortunately, the image fit, and the laugh sent poor Sidney into a tirade of tears.

That was long ago. She hadn't realized how much she depended on her husband to keep conversations going with Sidney. When had they quit really talking? When had they lost their connection?

Sidney woke up the next morning expecting a regular day. Her mom had quilting circle; Dad was going to be helping a family friend move into a retirement condo community. Mitchell wouldn't stick around to hang out with his boring, pregnant sister. Jon had a meeting that evening, and he'd be working all day. She was expecting nothing but quiet solitude.

"Good morning, sunshine," her mom chirped from the kitchen. Sidney's eyes went straight to the grandfather clock in the hall.

"What are you doing home?" she asked, surprised.

"Oh, I decided I could quilt just about any old time, but how often do I get to spend an entire day alone with my only daughter?"

"An entire day?" Sidney repeated, looking around for someone to rescue her.

Mrs. Flannery was immune to her daughter's less-than-favorable reaction as she rinsed her coffee mug and put it in the dishwasher.

"Yep," she answered. "I'm all yours, baby!"

"What did you have planned?" Sidney asked nervously.

"Why don't you get dressed, and you can find out."

Forty minutes later they were out the door. Sidney ate a bagel in the car since Mom seemed anxious to get going.

"Do you have a sign for the car with you?" Mom asked as they pulled into the parking lot of the mall.

"What do you mean?"

"You know, so we can use the pregnant mom's spot with the stork picture on it." She pointed at the empty spot.

"We don't need a sign, Mom. I'm kind of the proof. I'm not sure this is the best idea. I'm supposed to be limiting my activity, remember?"

"Pish-posh. Don't worry about a thing. If you can get yourself to those doors, I'll get a wheelchair for you. I promise I won't pop any wheelies."

Sidney waddled her way inside and waited on a bench while Mom got the wheelchair. She tried not to be embarrassed as she slid into the seat and let her mother push her toward the department store.

"You will be a mommy soon. There are a few things you'll need."

"Like what?"

"Like a crib, clothes, diapers. Honey, are you prepared at all?"

"Hmmm, I don't know, Mom. I've been a little preoccupied—trying to keep the baby alive and inside of me!" she snapped.

"You don't need to be so grim, dear. Expect the best, and good things will happen."

"That's not always true," Sidney said humorlessly. She didn't mean to sound hopeless or unhappy, because she wasn't. But it simply wasn't true that things would work out just because she wanted them to. She knew enough about life to know differently. There was something she never understood about Christianity. It seemed that an abundance of Christian believers went about life praying and expecting the perfect answers to their problems and they would get their prayer answered because they had positive attitudes, they believed enough, and they wanted it badly enough.

God forbid that it might not go as they'd expected and God in His infinite sovereignty had something better or even something different in mind for them. What was that all about? Did God misunderstand the prayer? Maybe He took the day off. Maybe He wasn't real at all. Anything could be true except that God had allowed the "imperfect" to occur.

Sidney had witnessed so-called believers lose their faith when they didn't get their way. She had been with a man who had buried God and his son the same day. She wasn't willing to be so inflexible. If God would just forgive her, she wouldn't ask for anything more. She probably didn't deserve anything more.

Jon watched the clock all day; each task he completed brought him closer to his six o'clock meeting. For an entire week he had prepared for this meeting. He had planned it out in his mind down to the smallest detail. He set the time two days ago, marking his calendar with an asterisk. The wheels had been set in motion long before that. If he really thought about it, it was years in the making. He reserved a table at a family-owned restaurant close to work.

By 5:45 he was pacing in his office, watching the driveway across the street, waiting for the blue Taurus to pull in.

Ten minutes later he spotted the car. He grabbed his coat, pulling it on as he locked up. As he raced into the restaurant, he felt his heart racing inside him. Was this an appropriate meeting place? Should he have chosen a more formal spot? Or maybe he was being too formal by choosing a restaurant at all. Maybe his apartment would have been a better choice—more personal, even vulnerable.

It was too late now. He ran his coat sleeve across his brow and took a deep breathe.

"I'm meeting someone," he told the hostess as he pointed at the booth in the back corner.

"The fun has arrived," Jon teased as he slid into the booth.

The waitress came back with two glasses of brown liquid.

"I ordered us each an Arnold Palmer," he was informed.

"Oh, well, I don't drink alcohol," Jon stammered.

"Neither do I," Mr. Flannery laughed. "You look like you could use some loosening up though."

Jon looked at the glass and back at the waitress, who smiled pleasantly as she explained that the drink was made of lemonade and iced tea mixed together.

She left them to decide on the menu while Jon settled his nerves with a sip.

"Is this a celebratory meal?" Mr. Flannery hinted.

"That would depend on you." Jon smiled and set the velvet box on the table beside his trembling hands. Mr. Flannery picked up the box and eyed the exquisite ring inside.

Jon slid his hands onto his knees and leaned back. He hadn't entertained the possibility of being told no.

"Well, I'm already taken," Mr. Flannery joked. "But I do know a pretty young woman your age who would be very pleased to slide this rock on her pudgy, pregnant finger."

"You think she'll like it?" Jon asked expectantly.

"I think she'd be crazy if she didn't. She's going to say yes, Jon. I know she'll say yes. Are you sure it's what you want? She doesn't come alone."

"I love her, sir. I can't stop. I've loved the baby too, more than its dad has."

"Has she been up front with you about that?"

"She has," Jon answered.

"Really?" Mr. Flannery asked, "You've known about the father?"

"He doesn't want her back, sir. I can promise you that. He looked pretty wrapped up in his own life, if you ask me."

"You met him?"

"He was a moment in her life, sir. I want to be her future."

"You have my approval. I'll be proud to call you son."

Mr. Flannery was a peacemaker, a fixer of sorts. He enjoyed life best when everything was in its place. He wanted his family happy, safe, and provided for, and he worried when something rocked that boat. He liked being a hero, the one with answers that would make it all okay. What man didn't?

After his meeting with Jon, he was filled with confidence in his parenting abilities. In just one day he'd managed to adjust both of his children's futures for the better.

Sidney would have a daddy for her baby, and she would be with the man she loved. All she had to do was say yes and slip on that shiny diamond ring. It was a pretty ring, the kind of ring that made him feel guilty for not spending more back when he'd proposed. But Mrs. Flannery wasn't the type to be impressed by a ring. He knew what she needed had just taken place. Sidney was going to be okay, and his wife could relax.

And life was going to fall into place for Mitchell as well. Yes, this was a good day.

Mr. Flannery had never had the patience that parenting Mitchell required. Mitchell's easygoing attitude must have been a random fluke trait that surfaced only once in hundreds of years of genetic make-up. Mr. Flannery didn't understand it, and he didn't have the time to waste watching Mitchell drift. Mitchell loved life, but he didn't trust himself to live it. It had been time for intervention.

Mrs. Weston had been a family friend for years. She was like a big sister to Mrs. Flannery and had introduced the two of them, promising the match to be perfect. And it had been a perfect match. Mrs. Weston was looking older these days, and the years had given way to arthritis and other ailments.

She knew it was time to move out of her beautiful, historic home in the heart of the city. She couldn't maintain it anymore, truth be told, and it was becoming harder for her to maintain herself as well.

Mr. Flannery had helped her pack up her belongings and move most of them into a storage unit. The rest he moved to a one bedroom condo. It was drastic downsizing and an emotional day for Mrs. Weston. Her childhood home would become a restaurant. There would be people drinking wine and twirling pasta onto their forks in the very spot where her mother had read her bedtime stories. She was too old for sentiment, she had told him, but he saw the way she paused in the doorway. Her hand caressed the doorpost in a silent good-bye.

"I won't let them tear down your memories," the new owner promised. "It will be beautiful, like when you were a girl."

Mrs. Weston smiled. "That was a long time ago."

She handed the keys to the young woman and didn't look back. She'd have kept her eyes fixed forward if that young woman hadn't tapped on the window just as Mr. Flannery slid the car into gear.

"Is there anyone you know, Mrs. Weston, who you would trust to make the adjustments to the house?" the woman asked. "I know you love this place, and it's hard for you. But if there were someone you know who you feel would be right for the job, I'd love to have a name."

Mr. Flannery spoke up. "My son is an architect. He grew up visiting this house and loves it as if it were his own. I think it's why he got into architecture in the first place." He scribbled Mitchell's name and number on the back of an old bank envelope and handed it to her.

"Tell him I'll be in touch. My name is Nicky." She took the number and smiled reassuringly at the stoic old woman in the passenger seat.

If there is an award for best father, surely it would belong to me today, Mr. Flannery thought as he poured himself a cup of coffee and tried to ignore his wife's curious stares. If she could take sole credit for their birth, then he was not giving this up. She could find out with the rest of them. Maybe when she did find out she'd bake him a carrot cake with cream cheese frosting. His stomach growled. *Oh, it has been a good day.*

Nicky waited a week before dialing the number. She needed the time to pack up and move into the house. It was then that she realized how little she'd actually brought with her.

Brad took a couple days off work and rented a U-Haul. Daryl, who lived across the hall from her apartment, provided him with months' worth of nonessential mail. He had been forwarding the important stuff. Daryl lent his muscles to the cause and helped wiggle Nicky's couch out of the door and down the stairs of her apartment. He had been a good neighbor, almost fatherly at times. His presence made her feel safe as a single woman coming home after dark. She would miss him.

It was good to be surrounded again by her things, even if they did look slightly modern in their new setting. And it was good to be on her own again. She loved the privacy and the solitude to read and reflect.

Nicky hated to admit it, but she liked Jennifer so much better when there was a little space between them. They were the kind of friends who were not meant to live under the same roof. Their friendship was a novelty, and the constant presence was slowly letting the air out of their balloon.

She would certainly not miss Brad's trail of cologne hovering in the air like a rain cloud. His morning muffins and espresso were nice, though. She missed being asked for a nine-letter word for housewives so he could complete the crossword puzzle in the back of the *TV Guide*. He made her feel smart when she felt she had made the stupidest decision of life. He left his socks on the floor of the bathroom, and even though it sent Jennifer over the OCD edge, it was worth it. He made her feel comfortable, and she found security in the little spots of imperfection.

She had shown Brad the number before she called it and felt some sense of relief when he recognized the name. He said Mitchell attended their church. Brad had played with him on the church softball team a few years back.

"He's pretty young," Brad told her. "I mean, he's like our age or close to. He's not some old guy who's going to have a huge history of the place."

"He was a family friend, though, right? He hung out here sometimes as a kid?"

"Yeah, it's worth a shot," Brad said with a nod of approval.

Mitchell answered the phone on the third ring. He'd raced up the stairs from the basement where he was sanding an old cradle he'd planned to surprise his sister with.

"Hey," he answered in his distracted way as he shook the sawdust off his shirt into the wastebasket.

"Is this Mitchell?" Nicky asked.

"Depends who's calling," he answered in his best mobster voice.

"Your father gave me your number. He said you might be interested in helping remodel the old Weston estate."

"Did he! I thought it was going to be turned into a restaurant or something."

"Well, yes, but…"

"I mean, I don't know anything about designing restaurants, and I'm not sure I want to be part of turning it into something it wasn't meant to be. I'm sure you guys make great food and all, but that's the place I learned to play jacks and marbles from Mr. Weston himself and where I caught my sister getting her first kiss in the broom closet during one of Leslie Weston's Christmas parties. It's got history for us, you know?"

"I was actually counting on that," Nicky answered. "We don't want it to lose its heart or its history. That's why we need someone like you, who remembers what it used to be and can help us revive the place."

She could sense his hesitance and continued, "Bradley Frank is the owner. He says he goes to church with you. I'm his wife's best friend, and it's really important to them that this place works. I'm like you, though. I'm looking at this beautiful carving in the door of an upstairs bedroom. It looks like it took forever to do it, and I wonder who made it and why the others aren't like it."

"That's easy." Mitchell chuckled.

"Maybe for you," Nicky continued.

"You really care about its history?" Mitchell's interest piqued.

"I sure do," Nicky answered.

"Tell you what. I'm going to be at a party the Franks are going to on Christmas Eve. Why don't we get to know each other there and see if we can work something out?"

"Are you asking me out? Because I'm trying very hard to be professional here." She smiled into the phone.

"Call it what you want, but I know Jennifer, and that girl's got some hot friends! I'd be crazy to forget that."

"How do you know I'm not the chick she drags around to make her look good?" Nicky teased.

"Cause she's not like that. I'll take my chances if you will. What do you say?"

"I guess so. I mean, I'll probably be there anyway." She quietly laughed at her attempt at indifference as she hung up and turned to the giant mirror above the couch.

"Oh man!" she whined to her reflection and the bump protruding from her abdomen. "He's going to wonder about you, kiddo!"

Suddenly, hot chocolate sounded really good. With whipped cream and a cherry on top. And she insisted on some ginger snap cookies dipped in apple pie filling. She called Jennifer, who agreed to meet her in twenty minutes at Starbuck's with a box of gingersnaps and a Tupperware container of apple pie filling.

Chapter Twenty-Three

JON'S APARTMENT WAS decked out with garland and Christmas lights and a six-foot spruce draped in popcorn. He'd had some help with all of it. The holidays really seemed to make Sidney glow, and he couldn't say no to her enthusiasm. She'd filled the living room with bowls of tinsel and shiny gold ornaments that shimmered and glistened like the diamond in his pocket.

He couldn't take his eyes off of her, mesmerized by the dance of lights across her cheek bones. She was tired, he could tell. The smell of the candles was getting to her, and she was blowing them out with enough force to kill a forest fire.

Mitchell had driven her over, and he looked like he hadn't slept all night.

"She's driving me nuts, dude!" he confessed when she slipped into the bathroom. "She was like a drill sergeant last night baking these cookies for you. She kept me up till three o'clock!"

Jon laughed at the bags under Mitchell's eyes.

"It's not even close to funny!" Mitchell went on. "She actually trashed an entire batch of cookies because I left them in the oven five minutes longer than the directions said."

"Those five minutes could have destroyed everything," Jon laughed. "You're lucky the cookie sheet didn't explode!"

"Seriously! You know it's bad when Mom's trying to calm her down," Mitchell said emphatically.

"That *is* bad!" Jon agreed as he set out the plastic ware.

"Mitchell has a girl coming tonight," Sidney informed them as she returned to the living room.

"Shut up!" Mitchell moaned. He rolled his eyes at his sister.

"Oh, are you still bitter about your batch of burnt shortbread?" she snapped.

"Yeah, that's it," he answered. "Keep it up, and I'll relight those candles."

"You wouldn't!"

"Dare me!" Mitchell cackled, lifting the matches over her head as she jumped at his hands and poked his ribs.

The buzzer signaled the arrival of guests, and Sidney seized the moment and grabbed the matches.

Joey waited in the hallway, letting his girlfriend enter first. Sidney took her coat and bolted to the bedroom, where she wished herself invisible.

"Jon, this is my girlfriend, Kristen," Joey introduced.

"May I?" Kristen asked, motioning to the back room.

"Yeah, sure," Jon answered.

"Do they know each other?" Joey asked once she was out of earshot.

"Beats me," Jon answered. Both men started down the hall, curious.

Kristen tapped on the door before entering.

"You okay?" she said. "If this is awkward for you, we can leave."

Sidney sat tall on the bed, posturing herself for bravery.

"It's really weird. I know it is," Kristen admitted.

"You have no idea," Sidney said. "This is a mistake I can't erase regardless of how hard I try."

"That's the thing about life," Kristen agreed. "We don't get to erase it. We just live it and keep moving forward."

"But it keeps following me," Sidney said.

"Yeah, I guess it seems that way."

"This is my boyfriend's place," Sidney offered.

"Oh."

"Yeah, he's terrific and I'm happy. Then I see you and I feel as if I don't have a right to any of it."

"Thank God we rarely get what we truly deserve," Kristen said. "I don't know what kind of mess I'd be living in if it weren't for grace."

Kristen sat down beside Sidney on the bed "You think maybe there's a reason God keeps throwing us together?"

"Morbid curiosity? A bias toward the ironic?"

"Maybe. Or maybe He wants to teach us forgiveness."

"It isn't yours to forgive. I broke your sister's heart, not yours."

"You broke your own heart. Alexis' heart was broken long before you," Kristen told her. "Look, let's just agree to have fun tonight, okay? Forget the history and accept that we're humans."

"Humans who screw up everything we touch," Sidney pouted.

"No, we're humans Christ loved enough to save from their own stupidity. Have you asked His forgiveness?" she asked hesitantly.

God used Kristen right then to relight the spark of hope that had been out for years. Sidney and Kristen prayed together, deaf to the arrival of guests and the chatter that was filling up the place. Peace washed over Sidney that went deeper than the warmth of the season. She was His again, and all the guilt and fear and anxiety were His to carry.

Nicky arrived with Brad and Jennifer, looking terrific. Mitchell introduced himself, offering her a shortbread cookie and boasting that he made them himself.

"Yeah, he made them under threat of death," Sidney added from the kitchen.

"My sister is a slave driver," Mitchell explained. "She's very pregnant, ready to pop any time now."

"Lucky for you Nicky's spent a lot of time researching the Underground Railroad," Brad said as he joined the conversation. "She could probably smuggle you right out of here and Sidney would never find you!"

"I should be so lucky," Sidney muttered. It was obvious she wasn't feeing well and was not at all herself.

"Why don't you sit down? I'll pass these around," Jon offered, taking the tray of cookies from her.

He knew the time was right to pop the question, but he needed a little help in pulling off the surprise. He motioned to Joey to follow him into the bedroom.

"I plan to ask Sid to marry me tonight," Jon confided. He tied a string onto a piece of mistletoe and fastened the ring to it as he talked. "Can you hang this for me? Be really subtle. I don't want her to notice the ring until I point it out."

"Not a problem," Joey assured him, taking the mistletoe and heading back to the living room.

Jon had planned the perfect romantic proposal. Sidney was standing right under the mistletoe Joey had managed to hang a few minutes earlier without a clue that her future was dangling right above her head. Suddenly she gripped the wall and held her breath. Every eye in the room turned to her.

"Call Mom!" she ordered Mitchell between pants.

"Forget Mom. Don't you think we should call the doctor?"

"I… want… my… mom!" she yelled, slamming the phone into his hand.

Mrs. Flannery spoke into the phone calmly and soothingly while timing Sidney's moans with the microwave clock.

"Honey, you need to go to the hospital now," she said in an encouraging tone. "Daddy wants to talk to you a second."

Mrs. Flannery handed the phone to her husband and began gathering Sidney's hospital bag and their coats.

"You're going to do great!" Dad beamed into the phone "Did Jon ask you yet? You said yes, right?"

On the other end of the phone Sidney's mouth dropped open. She turned to stare at Jon. She followed his eyes, which were fixed right over her head, and she caught sight of the glistening ring hanging in the mistletoe.

"Hello?" Mr. Flannery spoke into the silence. "Honey, are you there?"

Chapter Twenty-Four

ALEXIS SMILED DOWN at Christian as he brushed his fingers across her chest. She loved the closeness of nursing him. It gave her a feeling she couldn't explain. To call it love didn't seem big enough to match her emotions. He needed her.

Alexis and Peter had purchased Christian's first Christmas ornament a week earlier. They bought it at a kiosk in the mall and had it personalized with a gold-paint pen that made an eight dollar slab of clay seem like a real bargain. She could probably have done better herself. She had made Zeek's first ornament.

She would have captured the brightest star in the galaxy for Zeek if she'd had the tools. He made her forget that she was only a human and incapable of perfection. Pleasing him, loving him, had consumed her. Slowly, over time, Peter had disappeared.

This time things were different. Christian was loved fully and had her attention and would know the security of two committed parents. Alexis had learned that real love didn't need to be proven—it was simply experienced. It was so strong and so real that it didn't require an act—or an ornament—to be understood. Zeek's ornament hung next to his brother's, and that was okay. Each was precious in its own way.

She and Peter were exhausted. They had forgotten how tiring caring for an infant could be. Christian was nearly two weeks old before his parents realized the meaning of his name: follower of Christ.

They hadn't followed Christ in years. It seemed easier to rely on their own strength, at least in the beginning. They made God the target of their rage, their confusion, their blame. He was the one they could kick and scream and fight against. He allowed the slaps to His sovereignty, the attacks on His goodness.

Alexis had been angry and afraid, desperate and lonely, so she kicked at their circumstances. She and Peter had both become tired from fighting what couldn't be changed.

She finally called out to God for a solution. She had stretched herself so far trying to fix things that she had collapsed in despair. She was ready to throw in the towel when a brilliant light pierced through the wall she had built to protect herself, and she knew. She knew they would never be the same.

Things were different now. She and Peter were attending a church nearby, and they had hope again.

Alexis hadn't *really* celebrated Christmas for a long time. She blamed the Baby for stealing *her* baby away. It was like medicine to her heart when she unwrapped the Nativity set that had been stored away for so long. She slid her fingers over the figure of the Christ Child and wept.

"Thank you for your Son," she whispered. "Take care of mine."

Peter stood watching her and rocking Christian. His wife looked beautiful kneeling there by the Christmas tree, and he bent down to kiss her head.

The phone rang, and Alexis and Peter were prepared. They were ready for the news of the arrival of a baby girl named Ava Jillian Flannery. The little darling was born at 11:58 p.m. Christmas Eve.

She would never be a mistake. She was welcome.

Peter and Sidney talked for an hour. He listened to the details of Ava's birth and the description of every inch of her body. Sidney was proud and strong.

She told Peter that Ava was beautiful. Her wiggling infant form had proven just what an earlier amniocentesis had predicted. Ava lacked any visible defects. Every finger and toe had been accounted for. Her features were like her mommy's except she had Peter's eyes.

The doctor had scheduled an echocardiogram immediately after birth just to be on the safe side. It confirmed that Ava's heart was also healthy and strong.

Peter breathed a sigh of relief.

At last, Sidney said what needed to be said.

"Peter, we've both moved on. I'm with someone else, and we're going to be married."

"Congratulations," he answered.

"I want Ava to call him daddy. He's going to be with her, you know."

"Whatever you want, Sidney, but I'd like to know her. I want that. I don't regret her."

"Merry Christmas," she said before ending their talk.

It seemed that God hadn't been too busy restoring Sidney's hungry heart to also work a healing rhythm into little Ava's heart. God really was big enough. She sat for a moment holding the silent phone and reflecting on the way God had worked everything out for her benefit.

She would be okay after all.

She lifted her hand and smiled at the ring on her finger.

"Ava, your daddy picked a beautiful ring."

Chapter Twenty-Five

THE EXPANSION OF Portabella's required more hard work than anyone expected. It was a slow process. In January, they painstakingly repaired the woodwork in the dining room and repaired the windows in the ballroom. The hardwood floors were polished in February. The work brought Mitchell and Nicky together on a fairly regular basis. Nicky was due in March, and Brad was preoccupied with Jennifer and her anxiety.

They knew the baby was a boy. That had been unmistakable on the ultrasound. Jennifer had decorated the yellow nursery in a frog and princess décor. It was fitting. She was, after all, a princess.

Nicky was ready to be done. She had found someone who made her laugh and helped her approach life less seriously. They were working in the hallway upstairs one day. Mitchell was sanding the banister and Nicky was resting in the doorway.

"You never asked me to tell you about the door," he noted.

"What do you mean?"

"Remember when you wondered why that door was carved and detailed and the others weren't? Do you still want to know why?"

"Yeah," she answered, sitting down on the top step and motioning for him to sit beside her.

"Mrs. Weston was a writer you know, and she spent years encouraging her husband's work. He wanted to give her something really special to show his appreciation for her support, so he began to secretly work on the carvings in his shop. One day she came home from visiting a friend and she saw the door like this. She went inside and found that he had turned their guestroom into her library. She did all of her writing in there. It was her sanctuary."

"Really?" Nicky stared at the door. "Help me up. We need to go somewhere."

"Where?"

"We need a desk. The room shouldn't be without a desk."

"Okay," Mitchell said. "But now?"

"Yep." She waddled down the stairs ahead of him.

They agreed to go to a furniture store that sold unfinished pieces so they could embellish it and make it as extraordinary as the door itself.

Mitchell stopped at the red light and tapped on the dashboard, waiting for the light to turn. The light changed, and he inched forward to make a turn.

It was all very fast. So fast he would hardly remember it. He did remember the sirens and the flashing lights, the crunching noise, and Nicky's scream.

Jennifer and Brad thought Kristen was calling with good news when the hospital's number came up on Caller ID. Maybe it was time!

"I need you to come down here," Kristen said, only there was no joy in her voice. "Joey is on his way to pick you up."

"I can drive," Brad answered.

"Brad, you shouldn't drive," she insisted.

He looked at Jennifer, watching her face shift in confusion.

"What is it?" he asked. Jennifer took his hand and leaned her head against his to listen.

"There's been an accident."

Nicky had been silent and withdrawn, staring at the small, black speck on the ceiling above her. *This isn't how it was supposed to go. Why did this happen? I've gone through too much—given up too much—to be here in this place. It wasn't supposed to end with this heartbreak.* Did she have the right to grieve? She wasn't really his mother. She never planned to be. Now it wouldn't matter. It was all for nothing. It *couldn't* be all for nothing.

Jennifer entered the room and their eyes met. They held out their arms to each other and held each other close, tears dampening their shoulders.

"It's okay," Jennifer repeated again and again into her best friend's hair.

"It wasn't for nothing," Brad added, standing close to them. "He mattered. He had a purpose."

The three of them stayed together, holding hands for nearly an hour until the tears and medication finally exhausted Nicky. She fell into a deep sleep, leaving Jennifer searching her husband's eyes in bewilderment.

"This isn't the first baby we've lost. Why does it feel different?" she whispered.

"I don't know," Brad answered. "We had too much time to dream about him. He felt real."

"He *was* real."

"I don't know what to do," he quietly admitted.

Jennifer walked around the end of the bed and held him.

"He was going to have my dad's name." Brad pressed his face into her chest, and she felt his sobs shake his shoulders.

"They'll take good care of him," she answered, as she pulled him closer and rubbed her fingers through his hair.

"I love you so much," he said. "We'll get through this." He wiped her tears with his thumbs.

They sat together in silence for a long time.

Finally Jennifer said, "I need some time. Will you stay with Nicky?" She hoped he would understand. He did, and she slipped quietly out of the room.

Jennifer walked down the long hallway to the gift shop. She stared at the display window that held teddy bears in pink and blue and helium balloons with various sayings.

There wasn't one that said "sorry for your loss." She went into the shop and walked down the greeting card aisle, wondering if Hallmark had something to commemorate moments like these or if they were better forgotten. She found a notebook covered in lipstick kiss marks, probably left over from Valentines Day. She picked it up and examined the blank pages, remembering the laminated kiss she'd given the doctor at the beginning of this journey.

Jennifer bought the notebook and a pen and carried her purchases to a waiting room where she poured out her heart on the page.

She began to write, picturing him in her mind… Sullivan Joseph Frank…

I lost you today, and I can't understand why. I wanted you so badly! I was shocked when Nicky agreed to carry you. She did her best, you know. Your daddy would have been your hero. I know it. He loves kids. We both do. We love you. It was supposed to be different. We were going to get a call saying Nicky was in labor, and we'd rush up here to be with her and meet you and watch your first breath. Your cry would be beautiful. This silence is killing me. I was going to hold you and promise you everything. I'd have come through for you too. You were my dream. I don't know what to say to your daddy.

I don't know how to make it better or if there is even a way. I don't know what to say to Nicky. She gave up everything for us. You were hers, too, you know. She didn't really know how to love like this before you. She kind of did her own thing—she squeezed people in when it suited her. But she opened her life to you. We told her that you had a purpose, that your existence was for a reason, and if I had to pick one reason it would probably be her. She is so different now, Sullivan. She'll meet you in heaven, and we'll all be together someday. I couldn't have said that nine months ago. She was here because of you. I want you here. I want this all to be different. I want to hold you, squirming and alive. I want to take you home and place you in the crib in your beautiful room where I planned for you and dreamed of you. It isn't fair. I want a do-over. I want this all to change somehow…

"I've been looking all over for you," Kristen said as she entered the room.

"Is Nicky awake?"

"No, I just wanted to check on you." Kristen sat down next to her. "How are you holding up?"

"I'm not," Jennifer admitted.

They held hands, and Kristen began to pray.

"God, I don't understand why you choose to give or to take away, or how you know when to do it either. A baby lost his life today, and we can't make sense of it. Help us remember that you know these circumstances. You have plans for us. Plans to prosper us, plans to give us a hope and a future. We don't feel hopeful right now. Help us. We don't know what the future holds, but we'll be okay as long as you're holding us."

Jennifer and Brad went home to an undone nursery. The walls were painted a soft cream, but the crib had been removed. The guys had taken care of most of it for them. Just like that, it was over.

After a while, life went on. The world didn't stop, even though, to them, it seemed to stop at times.

They clung to each other, refusing to be another couple that shatters in crisis. They would go the distance as long as they lived.

Nicky had it rough at first. She continued to live in the old Weston house. She needed her space still. She hung out at the hospital after she was released, and she waited for Mitchell to recover. In time, he did. In time, everyone does.

And sometimes—in time—there's even a surprise, as there was when Brad and Jennifer welcomed Sally Frank into the world sixteen months later.

In life, the world doesn't end when the egg breaks. Sometimes it's just the beginning.

WinePressPublishing
Your Book, Defined.
Since 1991.

To order additional copies of this book call:
1-877-421-READ (7323)
or please visit our website at
www.WinePressbooks.com

If you enjoyed this quality custom-published book,
drop by our website for more books and information.

www.winepresspublishing.com
"Your partner in custom publishing."

LaVergne, TN USA
24 February 2011
217802LV00002B/8/P